RICHEMONT, E.
To summon a spirit

COUNTY LIBRARY

Nottinghamshire
County Council
Community Services

Please return / renew by the
last date shown.

Books by the same author

The Dream Dog

The Time Tree

Twice Times Danger

Wolfsong

For younger readers

Kachunka!

The Magic Skateboard

The Stone that Grew

TO
SUMMON
A SPIRIT

ENID RICHEMONT

WALKER BOOKS
AND SUBSIDIARIES
LONDON • BOSTON • SYDNEY

To celebrate the lives of Elizabeth and Kenneth,
Constance and Arthur, and Ludwig and Emma

And for Alfie and Anna, the future

First published 1999 by Walker Books Ltd
87 Vauxhall Walk, London SE11 5HJ

This edition published 2000

2 4 6 8 10 9 7 5 3 1

Text © 1999 Enid Richemont
Cover illustration © 1999 Mark Preston

This book has been typeset in Sabon.

Printed in Great Britain by Cox & Wyman Ltd
Reading, Berkshire

British Library Cataloguing in Publication Data
A catalogue record for this book is available
from the British Library.

ISBN 0-7445-6979-6

PART ONE

CHAPTER ONE

I can just see my face in the bedroom mirror. Beyond the jampot of daffodils and the GET WELL cards, I make out my dark, worried eyes, and hair that always needs brushing: brushing and braiding and damping down.

I think I look awful, all moony-eyed and pasty. Glandular fever, Dr Roberts says, takes a lot out of you. I wish that included the spot on my chin.

I grin feebly at my joke. Then I wave at my reflection. Hello, me! Hi, Jessica Jenkins.

I finger the spot, then freeze. That *is* me. Isn't it?

Don't be stupid, Jess Jenkins. Who do you think it is?

But then whose are those other memories, flitting like moths inside my head? I ignore them. Then they pester me. But whenever I try to catch one, it just fades into shadows.

Ma's pulled down the blinds so I can get some sleep, but the cool spring light still comes sneaking round the edges.

I close my eyes and concentrate. Something tells me this time I've got to remember.

I've got to remember.

Only then can I forget.

I snatch at one of those memories and this time I hold it, and a picture starts growing inside my head. It grows and it grows until it's all around me, like a 3-D film. I can taste it, touch it, smell it.

And then I'm there.

Autumn...

Autumn. Nearly winter. Already the light is fading and the days are getting short.

Fog catches at my throat like the ciggie I once tried, and wilted leaves litter the pavements like soggy cornflakes.

It's late October – the month seems to matter. Why? Suddenly I feel troubled, insecure.

Late October...

I'm walking home from school with some people from my class. The newsagent's displayed his usual welcome sign: ONLY ONE SCHOOL PUPIL AT A TIME. Today it's my turn. I come out with a bag of fruit drops, a couple of Crunchie bars, two packs of bubble gum and some cheese and onion crisps.

Then they all start complaining, "Oh, Jess! You've got it wrong, you've got it all wrong! I asked for *bacon* crisps, didn't I? And it was a *Mars* bar, you twit!"

But my friend Paula slips her arm through mine. "Stop fussing, you lot," she says. "This girl's having a hard time."

Paula knows. I've told her. Not everything, but enough. Paula's OK. And you've got to trust someone, have some kind of friend.

Suddenly that picture's all gone.

But now I'm remembering how the bad times started.

CHAPTER TWO

It was over a year ago.

I'd just started at Lewiston Comprehensive. I hadn't tried for St Peter's because my dad taught there.

Things weren't very different from primary school. Ma still worked part-time so she could be around when I came home, and Dad was for ever rehearsing for concerts and shows. He had this steel band which sounded awful, but it *was* getting better, and he'd just been setting up a classical quartet.

Then the bad times began.

First, the music department at St Peter's had to close.

Cuts, and they said sorry, it should never have been allowed, but they'd give my dad great references. After all, he only *ran* it!

Dad was devastated: he'd been really proud of his work. They hadn't bothered much about music at St Peter's until he came. Now he started filling in forms, standing in line, sweating about interviews and even grumbling about racism.

Then Ma broke the news. She'd been offered a well-paid job in some snooty suburb (we didn't know she'd even applied).

"The place isn't bad," she told us. "Southwood. Leafy and healthy. Lots of parks." Then she looked at me meaningfully. "And it's got a good school."

It's true: we didn't learn much at Lewiston Comprehensive, but all my friends from primary went there.

So in February we moved.

We had to.

Ma even found us the flat – a semi-basement job with a long scrubby garden that sloped down to woods. It looked good at first, exciting even. I'd never lived in a place with a garden before.

We trooped along like lambs to the estate office to sign the lease, but the landlord quite plainly didn't like me or my dad.

Well, that was fine, because I couldn't stand him. And neither could Dad, we could all see that.

Mr Stourby, our landlord. Filthy rich. Did something dodgy in the City when he wasn't robbing the poor. I remember his trendy glass-roofed room full of amazing house-plants, and Stourby lurking, like a predator, behind his desk.

Ma didn't seem to mind him. "Takes all sorts," she told us primly.

OK, OK. But do they have to come with breath that smells of rotten cheese? Or pale, flabby hands with that thin icing of sweat?

"Not his fault," Ma pointed out. "It's just the way he's made." Ma always tries to see the best in people. She's a counsellor, she's got to – goes with the job.

So OK, all right, the poor bloke couldn't help it. But he might have thought better about dying his hair – thin, blackened strands parted just above one ear, and then plastered across his fat, shiny scalp.

Did he think it made him look sexy?

To what? A skunk?

But after a few months, even Ma had to admit it – Stinky Stourby really *was* as nasty as he looked.

When our heating broke down in April, he just didn't want to know.

The boilers are serviced annually at the beginning of October. You may, of course, have yours checked, at your own cost.

We found mildew on the bedroom walls: the paper that concealed it sagged, then peeled off. Draughts blew in through the rotten window frames, and a power switch failed, melting all the ice-pops inside our rusting fridge.

The electrician told us that the wiring was crazy. A danger, he said, to life and limb. We had to borrow money to pay him.

"I'm having words with Stourby," threatened Dad.

"Don't upset things," warned Ma. "I *know* you. Don't fly off the handle. I'll talk to him," she offered. "He's OK with me."

I suppose that was the beginning. Dad got livid, said a whole lot of things he'd never said before.

I took Ma's side, of course. Later on, I took Dad's. After that I stopped caring – they just seemed to *want* to hurt each other. When they weren't getting at me.

But it wasn't just Stourby and his rotten equipment. It was us. Things we'd once have joked about were becoming big issues. *Bad vibes*, Dad began calling what was happening. Ma'd tease him, *"Joe, don't be so superstitious,"* and then that would turn into another row.

I said nothing but, like Dad, I was beginning to feel it – something sinister that seemed to prickle along my spine, something that made me want to snipe at them, and hurt. And we'd once been such a happy family. Now that seemed like a bad joke.

CHAPTER THREE

We found some second-hand heaters and cleared up most of the mildew. Dad put damp-proofing on the walls and stuck back the paper. Ma and Dad still went on fighting. But the weather slowly brightened and things didn't seem so bad.

I'd made a few friends at Southwood School – not close friends, but friends – people like Paula. I'd even auditioned for the choir.

And there was one good thing about the flat – I could climb over our back fence and get into the woods. The entrance gate was actually just round the corner, but climbing over made the woods feel like part of our house.

July came.

School closed.

There was no money to spare for a summer holiday. I tried to fix a few things up with old friends from Lewiston, but I was already out of touch. Posh, someone labelled me. *Me?* That was funny.

We spent a week in Liverpool with Gran, then came back to the flat. But the minute we returned, we started squabbling again. There was something disturbing about that place, almost a sense of evil.

Evil? I grinned. Well, it did belong to Stourby.

"Bad vibes," said Dad again, as if reading my thoughts. "Bad vibes, and a lousy landlord. We should get out. Leave."

"We've signed on for a year," Ma would tell him. "And Jess is settled."

Then they'd start rowing again.

I remember that summer.

It was hot and sweaty, and the grass in the back garden turned to straw, and the three of us spread beach towels over bumps of dried-out earth and pretended we didn't care about not going on holiday.

And we went on fighting. Me against Ma, and Ma against Dad, then Dad shouting at Ma, and Ma suddenly slapping me, which she'd never done before.

"That's child abuse!" I can hear myself yelling. Which was stupid, really – after all, I *was* twelve.

I'm still twelve; won't be thirteen till next

week. And don't they say thirteen is an unlucky number?

One night, after another row with Ma, I dreamed I was drowning.

I remember that dream. *Shining waters, a lake, a lake where there should be trees. Suddenly fog, edges blurred, white smudged on white – where am I? Where am I? Reeds stiff as swords, I seem to step through soft ice. The shock of cold is like fire. I gasp. My mouth and nostrils fill with sour water.*

And in that sticky August dawn, I woke up shivering.

CHAPTER FOUR

Summer holidays were over and the new term started.

I was in the Second Year now.

Sometimes Paula walked home with me; she was in my class. She had funny ideas, but we seemed to get on. It was still summery-warm and golden, although dusk came much earlier.

We had picnics in the woods, Paula and me, bringing drinks and munchies down from the flat. She told me she was a radical feminist, whatever that means. I don't think even she knew: she just liked to talk. I let her words wash over me without really listening, watching a butterfly I'd never seen before...

I was beginning to think of those woods as mine.

I began to resent the chattering mums who pushed prams along the paths, and the dogs that ran round barking at squirrels. I found I was irritated by the kids who swung from branches, or yelled at each other, playing silly games. I began to think of them as trespassers. They had no right to be there. Paula was OK. She'd come by invitation. I seemed to think that was the way things ought to be.

Then I'd stop and listen to myself. Did I *really* think like that? Maybe my old friends were right – maybe I *was* getting posh.

But those woods felt so private.

And once the gates were locked, they really *were* mine; mine, and some weirdos who sometimes broke in. Yobs, stupid yobs. I never saw them, but I heard them, crashing about and giggling and yelling. If they were there, I'd go home. I don't ask for trouble.

But actually, I never strayed far from the fence. I liked to sit, thinking, just being by myself, listening to the night sounds, the rustlings and hootings, and looking at the sky through the patterns of leaves. There was this bird that warbled all by itself – not tweets or squawks or whistles, but a sound you could relate to. Until then, I'd never believed in bird-song: before, it had always sounded like noise.

It was Ma who spoilt things.

I'd been watching a hedgehog slowly uncurling (it's true what they say about night-eyes – stay out for long enough, and you really can see).

Suddenly Ma came down the garden, flashing her torch. "Jess! Jess!" she was yelling. For my laid-back Ma, she sounded quite manic.

The torchlight zapped over the fence and nearly blinded me, and my hedgehog rolled up, tight as a clam.

"What's the fuss?" I was furious.

Ma snapped out things about risks and stupidity. Did she think I couldn't take care of myself?

We shouted. We ranted.

Then Dad joined the fight and for once they agreed.

"Forbidden," they both told me, "after closing time."

Now that really got to me. I was twelve and *they* couldn't trust me! They bickered all the time, then treated me like a kid.

Maybe that was why I had the nightmare.

I couldn't stop thinking about my lost pleasures, the little sounds, the silences, that feeling of being in my own private space.

One night I woke up.

No, something called me, drew me...

I heard a faint, rhythmic shuffling sound, a *chuffa-chuffa, chuffa-chuffa*. Was our heating about to die again?

I pushed open my bedroom door and listened. I could hear my dad snoring gently in his sleep. I went downstairs. I could hear the fridge humming and the boiler gluggling.

Chuffa-chuffa-chuffa-chuffa... The rhythmic sound faded. Whatever it was had gone away.

I unlocked the french windows and stepped outside. The grass was damp under my feet and I vaguely remembered – but that was the *patio* and there should have been *concrete*. I stood for a moment just staring at a silvery glaze of moonlight over velvet-smooth grass. Then I walked down to the fence and it was so easy, like walking on carpet, no scratchy leaves, no brambles, no stones.

But there wasn't any fence, just tall reeds and shining water. *Water, where there should have been trees.* I could smell a faint, sickly flower scent. Then I turned and saw lawn all spread out before me, and there weren't any fences and there weren't any gardens and there weren't any houses...

That's wrong. There was one.

A dark shape in the distance, like some grand hotel, its windows glowing with a soft orange light.

Then something washed over me, something cold, evil, monstrous, and somebody grabbed me and held me down. Those yobs, I thought stupidly; they've got me! They've got me!

I screamed and I fought.

Then I saw it was Ma.

20

*   *   *

We talked about it afterwards, tried to get it sorted. You can't avoid post-mortems with parents like mine.

It was like a confession. They both felt so guilty.

"Sleepwalking." They sighed. "You've never done anything like that before."

Ma said it was her fault, it was her new job. She was getting too involved and neglecting her family.

Then Dad said it was all *his* fault – that he was no good. And that was complete rubbish because my dad's the best.

I got impatient in the end, because it was so obvious.

"If it's anyone's fault," I said, "it's old Stinky Stourby's." Then I put in something sneaky, which wasn't really true. I told them it also *could* be because they'd stopped me going to the woods after dark. I went on about my nature studies – the hedgehog and the bird and the time I thought I'd found a glow-worm. "If I promise," I bargained, "to stay close to the fence?"

They looked at each other.

"OK," conceded Ma. "But at least tell us when you're going. We could hear you yelling, but we couldn't find you anywhere."

"But I couldn't tell you, could I?" I was losing my patience. "It was a nightmare. I sleepwalked. You just said so."

Well, at least it stopped them fighting.

For a week or so.

Then the letter came, from old smelly Guess Who?

There have been complaints about the playing of musical instruments. This was not allowed for when we drafted the original agreement.
I have now had your lease re-examined, and regrettably will have to charge you extra to allow for the nuisance.

"He can't do that!" stormed Dad.

"It's his property," Ma reminded him.

"Does he mean my recorder?" It wasn't much of a joke.

"I'll kill the rat!" raged Dad, punching his hands and kicking chairs. I know how he felt because I'm that way, too. Ma's so *reasonable* sometimes that it drives us both crazy.

But towards the end of October, even Dad got sort of quiet. He'd done another interview – a school not far from where we lived. It would have been perfect, if someone else hadn't got the job.

"A white man," growled Dad.

"You can't *assume* that," reasoned Ma. "Schools aren't usually racist."

Then one night, he said it. "I'm getting out," he told us. "I can doss down with friends, play in bars and clubs, anything. But I can't go on like this; I'm just a burden on you two. It won't be for long, but I need to sort myself out."

Ma cried a lot that night.

I didn't. I'd seen it coming.

It wasn't Ma, I thought, or Dad, not even stupid racists.

It was that man. Stinky Stourby.

And for the first time in my life, I really wished someone dead.

Autumn.

Late October.

Nearly winter. The crisp leaves we'd stomped through now lay in wilting brown heaps, and a clammy grey fog was making me cough.

That was the day I told Paula.

"My dad walked out last night."

"So what's new?" sniffed Paula. "Men are rotten," she told me. "Not to be trusted."

I wasn't convinced. Things weren't that simple. There was a boy in the Third Year I could have died for.

And I did love my dad.

CHAPTER FIVE

November, November, rotten old November.
Sodden leaves dangling in a dirty grey gloom.

Dad's gone. Only for a while, I keep remind-
ing Paula, not wanting to give her something
to go on about.

But now the grey gloom invades me and I'm
morose and grumbly. Ma's irritable, prickly
and we snap at each other.

We're both missing Dad, but we try not to
mention it. He sends us cheques, he calls us,
and we fool ourselves he hasn't really gone.
Ma tries to act reasonable, as if it doesn't much
matter. She reminds me smugly: other people
have worse problems. Me, I don't really want
to know.

And for the first time, I'm dismissive of
Paula's wacky ideas. She looks wounded, so I
instantly say sorry. Right now, I can't afford
to lose anyone else.

December.

Suddenly the gloom's all gone and everything's blue, gold and silver. My breath puffs out like I've swallowed fire, and school noticeboards sprout cards about carol concerts and discos.

I didn't always keep that promise.

Well, it would have been daft to tell Ma each time I climbed into the woods.

Anyway, they closed at four-thirty – still *officially* daytime, even though it was almost dusk. And sometimes Ma didn't get back until six or even later, and I could hardly call her at work to say: "I'm going to the woods!"

I'd sneak over just after they'd rung the closing bell, and a few straggling trespassers were scurrying out. Most of the trees were bare by then, and open to the sky, but the ivies still clung darkly, showing wicked black berries, and the hollies humped like giant green hedgehogs spiked with scarlet beads.

There was a special reason for my going there now. Those winter sunsets were wild – barley-sugar orange streaked with purple, gold and crimson. All this I was after. I had a cheap camera – a long-ago birthday present – and school was offering a prize for the best winter snap. A fancy automatic – not bad, not bad. I'd already nearly used up a whole roll of film.

25

I was squatting, working on an unusual angle, when my boot scuffed up something that glowed poppy-gold. I picked it up, but out of range of the sunset the colour quickly faded to a dull pinkish red. I squinted at it in the twilight. It was a small piece of brick with a pattern of two little rosettes. It looked like part of a narrow border, crumbling at the edges where it had broken off.

Pretty, I thought vaguely, stuffing it into my pocket. Then I scrambled back over the fence. It was too dark, I'd decided, for world-class photography, especially with a camera like mine. It was then that I saw someone standing in our garden. Talk about trespassers!

"Hey!" I yelled, pretending to be brave.

It might have been a burglar but it looked more like a bag lady, with a billowing wrap over skirts and skinny boots. But when I got closer, I saw it was a girl.

She was all kitted out for some fancy-dress party, with a frilly cap over hair that was looped around her ears. I guessed she was about my age, maybe a bit younger.

"Wrong house," I told her. And she nodded, and left.

I followed her into the back room to let her out, but she must have gone through our flat like a streak of light.

I ran upstairs and checked on our two bedrooms. I even looked in the bathroom, where no one could hide. I ran outside again; maybe she'd doubled back and climbed into one of the gardens. I thought I heard a low, mournful whistle, then that distant *chuffa-chuffa*, like an old-fashioned train from a film. Thomas the Tank Engine, I joked, but I didn't laugh.

Instead, I shivered and locked the french windows. I suddenly felt cold. I suddenly felt scared.

TV and chocolate sorted me until Ma came home.

She gave me one of her bear hugs. "Had a good day?"

I didn't tell her. Ma had enough problems. Instead, I showed her the little flower brick.

"Nice," she murmured. "Where did you find it?"

"In the street," I lied. "On my way home from school."

Then she said something that didn't make sense. "It must have dropped out of someone's front garden wall."

I goggled. "Huh?"

Ma pulled off her woolly hat and fluffed up her short, reddish hair. "Haven't you ever noticed?" she asked me. "Lots of those little walls have patchwork bits of old brick."

Next day I looked, and she was right. There were chunks of brick with leaves, and bits patterned with diamonds. There was even a single carved stone flower. There were scrolls and beads and little chunks of brick border like the one I'd found in the woods. I dawdled, fascinated, and got to school late.

If only it would snow, I found myself thinking: it would make a fantastic photograph. I could see it – snow, like icing, on top; then the blackened bricks of a low garden wall with a shock-surprise chunk of pinkish brick leaves. Glossy magazine stuff – wow!

"Where exactly did those chunks of brick come from?" I asked Ma that night. "They look like pretty bits some kid has pushed in to fill up the gaps."

She thought for a moment.

"There might have been a big house," she suggested. "A long time ago, when the city was smaller. Then maybe the land it sat on got sold, and the house got pulled down. The developers would have moved in, and the builders might have used up some of those decorative bits of rubble."

"Developers?" I groaned. "Back then?"

"Oh, they've always been around, and they weren't all bad." Ma smiled. "Those big houses had become too expensive to run, and ordinary people like us were getting richer. And lots of them wanted to live in places like this – where the air was clean, but they could still get to their jobs in the city because there was a railway."

I wanted to find out more, but there was nothing more she could tell me. And she was just guessing anyway.

"Try the library," she said, and I really meant to.

Then all kinds of things happened and I forgot.

First the disco, and that boy and I got briefly together, but then he got together with lots of girls.

After that, I won third prize in the photographic competition. Free film for a year! Not what I'd aimed for, but at least I'd been placed. When Dad rang, I told him, and he sounded so proud – anyone would have thought I'd made off with an Oscar!

Then on Christmas Eve it *did* snow, and that snow seemed to work magic. Dad turned up with presents, and fixed the lights on the tree. And I just *knew* that he'd soon find a super job, that Stinky Stourby'd come round, licking our boots and begging our forgiveness, and offering us free rent for the rest of next year.

I just *knew* we were all going to live happily ever after.

Oh, Christmas, Christmas…

Dad stayed until New Year. Then he left again.

And the fairy lights went out and real life came back.

CHAPTER SIX

January was bleak, January was boring.

And Christmas was something that seemed years ago.

One night, as I turned on my radio before getting down to homework, I found myself drifting, thinking about those bits of patterned bricks and stones, and Ma's guess about a grand house that got pulled down. I touched my own piece of brick with the two little rosettes, and all at once, I remembered my nightmare – the lake, the spread-out lawn, that large building on the hill, and the scary bit when I was sure those yobs had got me.

The radio started pounding out the Number One hit. Then I suddenly thought of something quite silly. *Might that building have been the big house Ma had guessed at?*

It was a crazy idea, but could I have *dreamt* it?

I must have dozed and dreamed again because I could hear this dog barking, not far away, not outside in the street but somewhere really close.

Then I found myself in a sort of park, on a cold stone seat. It was quite dark where I was sitting, under a thick arch of leaves, but in front of me the grass was sugary with frost and the sky was that clear, cold blue you always see in skiing ads. Tall, wavy grasses fanned out above a gravel path, and a big evergreen – a cedar, I think – cast long, feathery shadows across the slope of a lawn.

The dog barked again, then growled and whimpered. I could suddenly see it – a small, funny mutt trying hard to be fierce. I heard a voice: "Be quiet, Bruno!"

And someone was there, sitting beside me.

She was all done up in fancy dress, just like that girl in the garden – a frilly cap, a shawl, thick white tights and long white pants with lace that stuck out below her skirts. And she was staring at me with those dark, frightened eyes.

"You came," she wavered, as if I was some kind of a ghost. Then she seemed to pull herself together. "Oh, spirit…" She sounded as if she was starting a speech. "I summoned you," she said, "just like Martha taught me." Then she drew back. "I suppose now you want my soul?"

Well, I've been called some funny things, but never a spirit. "Spirit yourself!" I said. "And keep your lousy soul!"

The dog growled again, but the girl looked puzzled.

"I summoned you," she repeated. "And you came. If you are not a spirit, then what are you? You have red in your hair: Martha said that's the sign of the Devil. And your skin is dusky, like a peasant's or a gipsy's, and you wear pantaloons." She suddenly looked excited. "Are you a freed slave? A heathen? From Africa or India? Do you worship idols?"

"My dad's black and British!" I exploded. "He was born in South London. And my mum's a redhead from Liverpool. It's no business of yours, anyway. You a racist or something?"

The girl's eyes suddenly brimmed with tears. "I beg your pardon," she said. "I didn't mean to offend you. I just needed someone." Then she faded, dissolved, wasn't there any more.

My room was, though.

There was my collage of magazine photos, and my music and my homework jumbled up on the bed. A few pairs of my knickers drooped over the side of a drawer, and my radio was *still* pounding out that tune – the same words, the same line, the same phrase of music. I don't even like it.

Funny, I thought. Are they just repeating it?

Don't they have anything else to play? I began to sort out my homework but I just couldn't concentrate.

Ghosts, I kept thinking. Could you dream them?

But I didn't believe in that nonsense, and neither did Ma. And anyway, it was only a daydream.

Yet that girl had seemed so real.

The girl I'd met in the garden had been dressed like that, and she'd seemed real, too. Was it the same girl? I couldn't remember her face; it had been too dark. Now *she* might have been a ghost. It would explain how she'd vanished – she could have just walked through our back room wall.

And then there was my image of the house, the lawns, the lake. It all seemed to connect…

Suddenly I knew I had to find out more.

Next day, after school, I did go down to the library.

"I'll come with you," offered Paula. So we rode there on the bus. I didn't really want her around – this was *my* business – but I couldn't make up a reason for putting her off.

I explained to the librarian what I was looking for.

"Local history…" She frowned. "Don't have too much on that. We've got some copies of one or two old maps, though."

Paula rolled up her eyes. "Boring, boring."

"No, it isn't," I said.

The librarian looked at me approvingly. "School project?"

I nodded.

Paula raised her eyebrows. "Oh, yes. Since when?"

We went into the Reading Room and mingled with the wrinklies. One of them glared at us as if we'd come from outer space.

Paula eyed me. "Do you mind?" Then she went off to browse.

Afterwards, I thought I'd know where to find her – in Politics or Gender Studies – but she was sitting at a table, halfway through a book. She went pink when she saw me, then closed it quickly. It was one of those slushy romances I think are a joke.

"Sexist rubbish," Paula sniffed, pushing it away.

I grinned but said nothing, fingering the magic stack of paper in my bag.

That librarian had been great.

Well, she obviously didn't meet many kids like me.

She told me I should try the Southwood Historical Society. It sounded seriously stuffy, but I took its number down.

She even helped me copy the maps (not easy, they were big) and let me owe her fifty pence for using the machine.

"Pay me back sometime," she said, "when you're rich." If she was waiting for that, she'd be waiting for ever.

But the maps had been fascinating and not at all boring.

The first one was dated 1912. I could just pick out our road, and the place where my school would be. There were still lots of farms, though, and woods that had now vanished, and a field with a duckpond where the supermarket's built. I'd remember that duckpond next time I went shopping. Maybe the ducks turned into ghosts and went round quacking in the night among the frozen peas and ice-creams and big bags of chips.

But it was the other map that grabbed me – the much earlier one – no roads or streets, but land divided into plots with numbers or names on them, and little dots for hedges and shaded lines for streams. There were cottages, stables, one or two pubs, something labelled BRICK FIELD and a few big houses.

Which one? I wondered.

But I already knew.

Nightingale Court, it was called, and it spread out across a hill. There was a big curved drive at the front, bordered with trees, and at the back a huge garden that ended in woods and a stream. There was a plantation unsurprisingly labelled PLANTATION and some

35

ponds or flowerbeds (it didn't say which). All the big trees were marked with small squiggly circles and all the winding paths were drawn with little dots. And there was the lake, curving back into woods.

Water, I remembered, *where there should have been trees.*

Had they drained it much later? The ground dropped quite steeply from the backs of our gardens.

Then I took a long, cool look at myself.

Jess Jenkins, I said, you're taking this too seriously.

There aren't such things as ghosts.

And daydreams – even *nightmares* – can't ever be *real*.

CHAPTER SEVEN

When I got home, I spread out my photocopies
– four pages to each map.

Ma came in while I was shuffling them
around.

"What's all this?" she asked, dumping the
shopping along with her briefcase. She acted
flattered when I told her – after all, the guess
about the big house *had* been hers. She helped
me hold a set of pages while I joined them with
Sellotape. Then we pieced together the more
recent map.

"Interesting," she murmured. "Oh, look!"
she said. "There's us."

But I was more anxious to show off the earlier one.

"1862!" exclaimed Ma, impressed. "Let's
see: the main road's still there, but nothing
much else..." She sighed. "Just look at the
grounds of those houses."

I plonked my finger on to Nightingale Court. "That's ours," I said firmly. "That's where those chunks of brick came from."

But Ma shook her head. "Nice idea," she said, "but a bit vague. I mean, there aren't any real landmarks apart from that road. Now if you had a modern map drawn to the same scale…"

"Where can I get one?" I blurted.

She laughed. "Jess, you're obsessive! And besides, you'd have to trace it so you could line the two maps up. Try the library again. You seem to have made quite a hit there." She took the bags into the kitchen and made us some tea. "Dad's coming for the weekend," she announced casually. "Says he's been short-listed for a fantastic job."

The prospect of having Dad around for two days or even longer drove out all my thoughts about old houses and ghosts.

I told Paula, boasting.

"Hmph," she trumped. Well, she didn't much care for her own dad so it wasn't too surprising.

On Thursday, Ma bought Dad's favourite fish and marinaded it in lime juice and spices. She even had her hair cut by a friend at work. She didn't have to do a thing – my dad's a one-woman man – but I hadn't seen her so happy since New Year, three weeks ago.

So when he came through the door on Friday, she was looking really sexy, in that grey silky shirt that slims down her hips, and the mother-of-pearl earrings he'd given her for Christmas.

I let them smooch for a while, then I grabbed my share of hugs. We lit candles and played some old tapes. I considered telling Dad about my ghost girl, but it didn't seem relevant right then. We fooled around and sang. It was like old times.

Then two bombshells exploded.

First, the grill wouldn't work.

After all that preparation, Ma just burst into tears. Then Dad began stomping round, cursing Stinky Stourby.

"The man's a miser!" he shouted. "The man's a crook!"

"We could cook the fish in the oven," I pointed out gently.

"If *that* doesn't blow up," bellowed Dad.

Finally we managed to put supper together, but most of that good feeling was already gone.

Then Dad dropped the second bombshell.

He'd been shortlisted for a great job – yes. Trouble was, it was a hundred miles away.

They argued.

We all argued.

"We'll move," said Dad. "No more Stinky

Stourby. No more lousy flat."

"What about Jess?" put in Ma. "She's had one move already."

"She's young and adaptable," said Dad. "Another move won't hurt her."

They were talking about me as if I wasn't really there, and that always makes me furious.

"I like my school!" I shouted. "Don't want to move to your rotten old country town. And anyway, what about Ma's job? She's got rights too, and no one's asking her!"

It went on like that all through the weekend.

It was just like old times, yes: awful, recent old times.

By Sunday night I'd had enough. I just stormed out.

I ran down the back garden and dropped over the fence. The stars were out and it was icy cold, but at least it was peaceful, at least it was quiet.

The universe... I thought, unwinding. Time and space and all that science fiction stuff, bigger than parents, bigger than me.

A cold breeze sputtered through dry, leafless branches and I suddenly smelt that cloying flower scent. I could hear a dog barking wildly; it sounded berserk.

Then all hell broke loose and terror seized me.

It was just like the nightmare, but I wasn't asleep. It was evil, horror, badness, all rolled into one. My head suddenly throbbed, then something icy went over me. I struggled against darkness and then I ran. I ran blindly, seeing nothing. Then I ran into daylight. It was like having the light switched on when I was still asleep.

I blinked and stood, rooted to the spot. And then I saw the girl, with her back against a tree. She had a bonnet and a cloak and those pointy boots, like ballet shoes.

"Oh, spirit," she began. But I was in no mood for her nonsense.

"Don't start that again," I told her. "I'm no different from you. Except I'm…" What? *Alive?* I couldn't say that. "I want you to tell me something," I added fiercely.

She stared at me, frowning.

"Something happened here," I told her. "Something bad."

She nodded. "I know." I hadn't expected that.

I was trying to work out how to tell her that whatever it was had happened a long time ago, that it was haunting me, that I came from the future.

But she stopped me.

"I am that bad thing," she said. "Else how could I have summoned a creature like you?"

Now that really annoyed me. I thought I was going to find out something important, and all she could come out with was that stuff again.

"I've told you," I snapped. "I'm just a girl. And I may pick quarrels, but I'm *not* an evil spirit."

She suddenly stood up and our eyes drew level.

"I am wicked," she repeated. "I am evil. I am bad."

I gave up. "So what have you done?" I asked feebly. "Apart from summoning me."

"I take Papa's books," she whispered, "from his study. And I read them."

I had to laugh. "That's not a crime."

Then she swallowed hard and her face went ashen.

"And I killed my own mother," she said. "That's why Papa hates me."

I backed off. I was shocked.

I had nothing to say, what could anyone say? She didn't look old enough to murder anyone; she could have been in my class at school.

Yet sometimes, I knew, even children could kill.

But all that frilly stuff, that fancy dress prettiness…

I stepped back. I had to.

I stepped back into darkness.

Then I heard voices – "Jess! Jess!" – and saw torches flashing. "Jess! Where are you?"

And suddenly Dad was there.

CHAPTER EIGHT

Things calmed down after that, and a truce was called.

Even the three battling Jenkinses couldn't go on for ever.

Ma finally pulled the heavy counselling string – that family conflict was disturbing for an adolescent girl. We'd had a boring heart-to-heart, with her asking pointless questions like: *Where on earth did you think you were going?*

"Away from all the fuss," I'd told her (if I'd mentioned ghosts, she'd have had me signed up with a shrink). If only I'd had a brother or sister, I thought for the millionth time, they wouldn't have had to concentrate so much on me.

I came close to it once. Maybe that was why Ma was so overprotective. She got pregnant again when I was about nine. Then she got ill,

43

and lost the baby. A little boy, she told us. My little brother. It was the only time I'd ever seen my dad cry…

So we'd decided.

If Dad *did* get offered the job, we'd all move. Rents would probably be lower, and we might even take out a mortgage on a house. With Dad working again, in that posh school's music department, it might be possible for Ma to set up her own private counselling practice.

But the best thing, we all agreed, would be telling Stinky Stourby what to do with his rotten old flat!

Yet it all floated past me without really registering.

I was still in shock.

Could that girl have killed her mum?

I'd always believed if someone was *really* bad, it would show. I mean, I didn't think it went along with being ugly – that's stupid. Horrible people can look quite ordinary or even attractive, and lots of kind, good ones can seem boring or plain. But I'd imagined there'd be a sort of coldness, a hardness, a brutality which that girl just didn't have.

But how could I be sure? I'd only met her twice (unless it had been her in the garden that night).

I went on working at it, like a sleuth. I just

couldn't let go.

How did someone kill someone? I listed the ways. They could shoot them, or stab them, or hit them on the head. They could strangle them or smother them, but soon after that, I ran out of nasty ideas.

"How would you kill someone?" I asked Paula.

She looked startled. "Have anyone in mind?"

"Stinky Stourby, our landlord," I told her. "He's a rat."

"Then rat poison," said Paula. She suddenly waxed enthusiastic. "Why not get him a big box of chocolates, and poison each one?"

A tempting idea, but they'd probably catch me! Poison was possible, though... That girl wouldn't have needed much strength or violence for that. Just hate.

"Where would you get hold of poison?" I asked Ma that evening.

"You couldn't," she said. "Things like that are strictly controlled. They weren't once, though... Those old Victorians could always nip round to the chemist and pick up some arsenic. Some of them even doped their babies with laudanum to get them to sleep."

"What's laudanum?" I asked.

"Opium," she said calmly.

And I'd thought drugs were something new.

"How does arsenic kill you?" I asked her.

"Slowly," said Ma. "It was their favourite way of doing in unwanted relatives." She gave me a hard look. "This is a gruesome conversation; were you thinking of me?"

"Oh, Ma!" I hugged her. "Don't be so silly!"

"Just wondering," she teased me.

But I didn't find it quite so funny.

That night, I couldn't sleep, just couldn't stop thinking. Maybe that girl's mum had been cruel and nasty. Some mums were; you read about them in the papers; maybe the evil I'd picked up came from her. Then I started wondering about her dad. I mean, what kind of a bloke would have shacked up with a woman like that?

After all, I had a right to know. If she really *was* a ghost, it was me she was haunting.

I reached out for my piece of flowered brick – pretending, like a kid, that it might carry me back. I played with it, and wished on it, but nothing happened.

At that point, I gave up.

So much for magic, I thought.

The following week, Dad rang.

He'd been offered the job!

We all went out to celebrate, although we couldn't afford it.

Away from the flat, we were relaxed and

happy, and over curries and poppadums we shared all our plans. I knew I'd miss my school, but I didn't make a thing of it. I knew Ma'd miss her job, but it was Dad we were both thinking of. Music was like his religion – it was what he most cared about, and he'd been playing in pubs and places where nobody really listened.

Ma said Stinky Stourby had to have his three months' notice, so we'd probably move out just before July.

Lots of time, I thought. It wouldn't take long to get hold of the right map. But how could I find out about the other things?

I might have more of those daydreams, but then I might not. And I *did* want to ask her, to understand.

Why? I suppose because I'd never known someone who'd killed – especially someone of my age. I was a bit like Ma – I wanted to get at the reasons. There *had* to be a reason: no one killed their mum for nothing, unless they were crazy. And I couldn't believe that girl was either crazy or bad.

Dad flicked his fingers. "Penny for them?"

"Oh, nothing much," I told him, spooning up my mango. "Just thinking about a ghost."

"If you've got ghosts for friends," joked Dad, "you don't need any enemies!"

I shivered. Maybe he was right...

* * *

I went back to the library to ask about a modern map.

I explained to the librarian what I wanted to do.

She shrugged. "That's a hard one. We've got an up-to-date survey map, but it won't have the same scale as your two golden oldies. You'd have to enlarge it or reduce it, and our machine won't do that."

I made some photocopies anyway and paid her this time. Then I remembered the other thing.

"How could I find out who lived in one of those old houses?"

"Try the Historical Society – they're into that kind of thing. They could probably help you with maps, too." She gave me its number again because I'd lost the first one. "If you need any more help..." She really *was* nice.

It took me days to pluck up courage to call the Southwood Historical Society, and then when I did, the phone just rang and rang.

So I looked up their address and sent them a letter.

I got one back within days. They seemed pleased that I'd written. They even asked me to their office to look at their archives.

But there it all was:

NIGHTINGALE COURT. BUILT 1828. COMPRISING 72 ACRES, TOGETHER WITH GARDEN, ORCHARD, STABLES, OUTHOUSES AND TENANT'S SMALLHOLDING.

FIRST OWNER, WILLIAM EDWARD BENTON, MERCHANT. SPOUSE, CATHERINE LAURA JAMES. M. 1837 DIED IN CHILDBIRTH, 1839.

ONE CHILD – LAETITIA CATHERINE. BORN 1839. DIED 1851.

I stopped reading at that point because the child's name grabbed me, I don't know why. There might have been other girls who'd lived in Nightingale Court, but I knew I'd found her.

It was that funny name, Laetitia. Like a sneeze, I thought. *Laetitia! Laetitia! I'm getting a cold.*

I began counting on my fingers. She'd been twelve when she died. Same age as me…

But something didn't quite fit.

Catherine Laura James, I thought. Died in childbirth. 1839? But that was when Laetitia was born, so how *could* Laetitia have murdered her mum?

Then I suddenly saw it. *They'd all blamed the baby!* That poor kid must have grown up thinking that she was a killer.

It was awful. It was frightful. And I *had* to tell her.

I had to go back and tell her that it just wasn't true.

CHAPTER NINE

It rained all that weekend.

Trapped inside the flat, Ma and I snapped at each other. Then she turned on TV, neatly shutting me out.

I went to my room and sprawled on the bed, browsing through the history book I'd borrowed from school. Being lazy, I picked out bits that had the best pictures, like Queen Victoria's wedding, and the Great Exhibition.

Then I found out there'd been a cholera epidemic.

Was that what had killed my friend?

Laetitia, Laetitia...

Had she lain in bed, feeling awful, thinking she was a killer? And they took religion so seriously – *had she believed in hell?*

And I'd discovered a few things from a science lesson at school. Mr Simms had been talking about germs and diseases – the link hadn't been discovered until quite late. People didn't fuss that much about cleanliness, and there wasn't any really clean drinking water, so women were dying in childbirth when all they needed was Dettol and some soap. He even gave it a name – puerperal fever. I wrote it down carefully, thought I'd use it to impress her.

If I ever saw her again.

Maybe she'd decided that I wouldn't want to know a girl who'd killed her own mother...

I fingered the flowered brick. I needed story-book magic. I had to sort out that poor kid before it was too late.

But she was already dead, wasn't she? And you couldn't die twice. At that point, my thoughts got tangled up and I started a headache. I went down for some aspirin and found Ma on the sofa, watching a boring old black and white film.

I looked at the screen. There was this glittery blonde, sobbing. Then the sound suddenly died and the picture seemed to freeze.

I groaned: something else that didn't work! And there was that late-night funny show I'd wanted to see.

I thought Ma'd be making a fuss, but she didn't say a word. She just went on staring at the screen as if nothing had happened. I gave up on her: talk about a zombie!

The french windows suddenly blew open

and I forgot about my aspirin. Fresh air was good for headaches and the rain had finally stopped.

The rain had stopped and a wild wind was blowing, making the curtains billow out around me like flowered sails. I stepped outside. The treetops were all swaying, and fine needlepoints of sleet blew into my face.

Then I noticed the trespasser in our back garden.

Her face was shaded by a bonnet, its long ribbons fluttering, and she wore a flapping cloak over the usual mass of skirts.

She came up to me slowly.

"*You* summoned *me*!" she said.

I began to laugh. "That makes *you* into the spirit." I suddenly thought of something else. "Would you like my soul?"

She stared at me, shocked. "I am *not*," she huffed, "a spirit."

"What are you then?" I teased her.

"I'm a young lady," she informed me primly.

"Young ladies have proper names," I said cunningly. "And spirits haven't."

"I'm Laetitia," she said. As if I didn't know.

It was totally childish, but I couldn't resist it. I put my finger under my nose and made that little kids' joke: "*Laetitia! Laetitia! I'm getting a cold.*"

She frowned. "How unfortunate." Then I

saw her mouth twitching.

Laughter is catching. Like a germ, but more fun. I felt my face creasing and the giggles fizzling upwards. Then I saw that the same thing was happening to her.

We went on and on, winding each other up. I don't think she'd laughed like that for ages, maybe never. And the wild wind rattled her bonnet, and tangled my hair and puffed out her cloak like a parachute sail.

And behind us I saw the lake fringed with reeds and rushes, its tinny-grey surface whipped up into points. A couple of geese swerved, then landed on an island. I started to shiver. *Water,* I thought, *where there should be trees.*

But there *were* trees, lots of them, all around it. A forest, or at least a big wood.

I turned away then, because that lake still bothered me, and saw the house, for the first time in daylight, all spread out on the hill, the smoke from its chimneys blown sideways by the wind. It was built in two parts, joined in the middle by a big glass conservatory, and its roofs were decorated like castle tops. It seemed much too big for just one family.

"Do you live in all that?" I asked her.

She nodded vaguely, obviously thinking of something else. "Spirit." She eyed me. "Do *you* have a name?"

This time I didn't get mad, because I could

53

see her grinning. "It's Jessica," I told her. "But everyone calls me Jess."

"In that case," she said formally, "you may call me Lettie." And she held out her hand, and I touched a ghost.

But her fingers felt quite solid, just thin and rather cold.

"Hi, Lettie," I said. Then I remembered why I'd tried to call her. "You told me," I reminded her, "that you'd killed your mother."

Her eyes seemed to darken under the shade of her bonnet.

"But you couldn't have," I blundered on. "You were only a baby."

I saw tears on her cheeks.

"They told me I tore her body apart," she whispered. "And she died in agony."

"Who told you?"

"Martha."

"Who's Martha?"

"My nurse."

I looked at her anxiously. "You're not ill. Why do you need a nurse?"

She seemed puzzled. "I don't have one now, of course. I'm no longer a child, I'm twelve. I have a maid, and a governess."

"So this Martha," I went on, "told you all those things when you were very little?"

Lettie nodded. "She knew lots of things. She knew how to charm warts and find out if someone was a witch. Once she tried to raise

54

Mama's spirit so that I could say sorry."

"That's awful!" I shuddered. "That's yucky! But where was your…" I struggled to say it, "papa?"

"He went away," she said. "You see, he loved Mama so very much. And when I killed her, he nearly died of grief. It was my aunt who took care of me. But what of you?" she asked, neatly changing the subject. She plucked at my jumper and fingered my hair. "You say you are a girl, yet you dress like a man. And you have coloured threads in your braids, and an uncovered head. What place, then, do you come from? And I *did* call you," she added stubbornly. "I *know* I called you…"

Her voice faded, and all at once, I heard someone else's. *"Don't leave me like this!"* It was the blonde on the screen.

I watched her lover shrug on his coat and slam the door – the film was just going on. It was as if nothing had happened since I'd gone down for some aspirin.

Ma shifted on the sofa and put down her knitting.

"What a day!" she grumbled. "Thank goodness for the telly."

Then I saw the rain streaming down the locked french windows.

CHAPTER TEN

I tried to work it out.

It was as if no time had passed in my world, as if nothing had happened, as if Lettie's world was going on at the same time as mine.

But that wasn't possible: she'd lived way back in the past. I still remembered the date, like I knew the date of my birthday – Laetitia Catherine Benton, born in 1839.

I didn't want to think about that second date. It seemed so unfair – why should Lettie have died before she'd had a chance to live? I couldn't wait to be officially grown up – no more fusses and rules, no more homework to do.

So in Mr Simms's class on Tuesday, I asked my mindboggling question: "Is time travel possible?"

He'd been talking about magnets, but he didn't seem too bothered. "It would be fun, wouldn't it? Go back to Good Queen Bess and all that. Quantum theory suggests there might be alternative universes..."

We all groaned. "Oh, no! What's that supposed to mean?"

"Something that even Einstein didn't properly understand." He shrugged. "You see, there's a problem. What if you went back and changed something accidentally? For example, supposing you turned up in someone's garden – let's say a young man's garden. Sorting you out might distract him from going to a party where he'd meet the girl he was going to fall in love with. Now if that young man had been your grandad, and that girl your grandma, they might never have met. So your mum or your dad would never have been born, and you wouldn't exist now."

I worked it out. It was complicated. It was creepy.

He had to be exaggerating.

I'd already spoken to Lettie, and I was still around, wasn't I? Anyway, she wasn't related to me, and she seemed a bit young to be going to that kind of party. And she was going to snuff it anyway, long before she grew up.

And I wasn't setting out to change anything *big*.

I just wanted my friend to die happy – no risks involved in that.

*   *   *

Dad planned to go on doing odd jobs until just after Easter. Then he'd go away and flat-hunt. After all, we wouldn't need a place for ages yet.

But old Stinky Stourby had other ideas.

We got a letter one morning giving *us* three months' notice. Seems he had plans to turn the house into luxury flats.

Even Ma went berserk. "That old lady upstairs!" she raged (although we didn't actually like her). "She's been living here for years, what's she supposed to do? We'll organize something, complain to the council!"

But I knew and she knew that we didn't stand a chance. Stinky Stourby was wily; he was probably *on* the council. All we could do was start looking for a temporary place.

"A bed and breakfast," wailed Ma, "and we can't afford it. But we won't find anything else for such a short time."

But I was more concerned about other things. Only three months; that gave me February, March and April, with still no guarantee of ever seeing Lettie again.

Maybe she'd go on haunting me, but maybe she wouldn't. At least the scary bit would go with her if she went away. She was a ghost, after all, so I supposed there *had* to be a scary bit. But I'd already grown fond of her. She was nice, she was funny, we seemed to laugh at the same things.

I dug out my letter from the Historical Society and went through it properly this time. I studied their list of the people who'd lived in Nightingale Court – it was really quite a short one.

I found out that Lettie's dad, William Benton, had died on some expedition. Then his estate had passed on to his younger brother, Charles. This brother Charles went off and married someone called Maria. Then brother Charles died, too, not very long after.

Busy, busy Maria, I thought: she didn't wait long, because there she was again, hooked up with this guy Greenwood, and having a daughter called Hannah, and a son who died. *In infancy*, I read.

They dropped off like flies, those Victorians, I thought.

After that, the estate got broken up, so the list didn't go on. But one extra thing the secretary did mention – the Benton family was buried in All Saints Parish Church.

I found it on the map – it wasn't too far away. Paula came with me – she liked funny old churchyards. I took along my camera because I did, too.

It was Paula who spotted it, enclosed behind railings – a big stone vase with carved plants, their stems and leaves falling romantically over an ancient stone vault. The vault was cracked, and blotched with lichen.

"Ghoulish." She sighed. "But I suppose there's no one left to look after it."

We managed to read the verse.

HOW LOV'D, HOW VALUED ONCE AVAILS THEE NOT
TO WHOM RELATED, OR BY WHOM FORGOT.
A HEAP OF DUST ALONE REMAINS OF THEE
'TIS ALL THOU ART AND ALL THE PROUD SHALL BE.

"Ugh!" shuddered Paula. "So what creep did it belong to?"

We walked round to the other side. Then she pointed. "Weren't those the people you were looking for?"

Then between us, we worked out most of the words. CATHERINE LAURA came first. CHERISHED WIFE OF WILLIAM EDWARD BENTON OF NIGHTINGALE COURT. BORN 1818. CALLED TO HEAVEN APRIL 17TH, 1839. "NO ANGEL HALF SO FAIR." When we came to LAETITIA CATHERINE, DAUGHTER OF THE ABOVE. BORN APRIL 1839. PERISHED (but the rest was covered in lichen) I nearly cried. We made out THE ABOVE WILLIAM EDWARD BENTON, BOTANIST, LOST IN NEPAL 18 (something-or-other), then CHARLES (something) BENTON (that must have been his brother).

I took a couple of photos I hoped would be atmospheric, then lent my camera to Paula. While she was busy focusing on a soppy- looking angel, I rescued a plastic rose from a pile of garden rubbish and threw it over the railings. It wasn't very grand, but at least it was something.

We bought a couple of buns and ate them on the way home. I didn't do much talking.

"Listen," said Paula, misunderstanding my silence. "Don't worry about what happens when that rat chucks you out. You can come and stay with us – we've got a spare room."

I was quite fond of Paula, but the idea appalled me. "Thanks," I said, my heart sinking. "That's really nice."

I went on home, unlocked the door and let myself in. I made some tea and ate some ginger biscuits. Then I glanced out of the window; it stayed light much longer now.

So I walked down the garden and climbed over the fence. *Haunt me! Haunt me!* I dared Laetitia.

I hung around until it was properly dusk. I heard the closing bell ringing and the trespassers leaving, then the woodkeepers' voices as they locked up the gates.

Soon after that, my special night bird started singing a solo I longed to put on tape. It would have made a good theme, I thought, to play on my school flute. I listened, and added drums and a soft tenor sax. Fantastic, I thought, impressed with myself. I always knew I was a musical genius!

The bird was still warbling when I noticed water lapping at the toes of my trainers. I looked up, expecting Lettie, but someone else was there.

A woman in mauve silky stuff stood, glaring down at me. She had a small, sensuous mouth, but what she said wasn't pretty.

"Gipsy!" she spat, as if it was a swear-word. "We've set man-traps, you know. And we'll have you vermin hunted off this land if we catch you here again."

She took one step towards me, then I smelt that perfume – that cloying flower smell from my nightmare that had made me feel sick.

I gasped for air, but began retching.

Then my hands reached out and found the fence, solid and *real*. I scrambled over it clumsily, tearing my jeans.

Then I struggled back to the flat.

CHAPTER ELEVEN

All that evening, I felt frightened and confused. I couldn't think about homework, and even the Chinese takeaway Ma'd picked up didn't appeal.

Could that awful woman have been Lettie's aunt? Had she found out that I'd been trying to tell her niece the truth? But whatever had happened back then wasn't Lettie's fault. How could it have been? She was only a baby.

That night, I tucked the brick flowers under my pillow, and called her silently, "Lettie! Lettie! Laetitia! Laetitia! I'm getting a cold!"

Did I dream it? I don't know, because it was beginning to be hard to sort out dreams from what was supposed to be real. I remember standing between two blackish green cones that almost blotted out the light.

Aliens, I thought. Then I reached out and touched one, and found it was a tree.

"Boo!" Lettie rustled out from behind it with her funny little dog. "Yews," she explained. "Josiah's idea. He's been trimming them like that for years." She pulled a face. "I think they're ugly. They used to frighten me when I was small."

I heard the distant *chuffa-chuffa* sound again, the mournful, fading whistle. I suddenly recognized it, from old films.

"Is that a steam train?" I asked.

She nodded. "Of course. Don't you have them yet? There isn't a proper station, but they're building one. My aunt and I go to the seaside once a year now," she boasted. "There's an excursion. Have you ever been on a train? It's the *only* way to travel."

I couldn't resist showing off.

"I fly," I said. (Well, I had once. To Ireland.)

But Lettie burst out laughing. "Show me your wings!"

"We have aeroplanes." I struggled to describe them. "They're like trains in the sky."

"Trains that fly? I don't believe you! Do you harness spirits?"

I giggled. "Lettie, there aren't any spirits."

"Then how do they work?" she persisted. "By steam? Tell me."

My cheeks flushed. I'd have to ask Mr Simms, because I didn't know.

"I met someone," I told her, quickly changing the subject. "A woman in a mauve dress and a flowered woollen shawl. Could that have been your aunt?" I shivered. "She called me a gipsy."

Lettie stared at me. "*Are* you?"

"No," I told her. "And I wouldn't want to be one with her around."

Lettie laughed. "I think that must have been Miss Hurst, my new governess. She hates gipsies." She paused. "Did she smell?"

I wondered what she meant at first. Then I caught on. "You mean, scent?"

"Yes. Violet cologne. She's got a big bottle in her room – I've seen it. She says she puts it on for gentleman callers, but there's really only one, and that's Uncle Charles. Do you have a governess," she twinkled "*demon* Jess?"

I shook my head. "I go to school."

Lettie sighed. "There was talk," she said, "of sending me away to school. But Aunt Harriet thought it might be a bad influence; she doesn't believe in too much education for girls. Then my uncle found me a governess, so it was no longer necessary." She curled her hand around her mouth. "I play tricks on her," she whispered. "I keep catching her out. She's stupid and vulgar. And she treats my aunt like a servant."

"What about your dad? What does he think about it?" She looked puzzled. I corrected myself. "I mean, your papa."

"Uncle Charles has not received a letter for several months. It is possible Papa is dead." Her face didn't change a bit when she came out with that.

I remembered the gravestone. "So you might be an orphan?"

She nodded calmly. "But I have my aunt and my uncle. And after all, I am well provided for."

I guessed she meant money, but I didn't dare ask.

We walked up three small stone steps and emerged into daylight. The small dog raced ahead, then came back dragging a stick.

"Oh, Bruno," sighed Lettie, pretending to wrestle it from him. Then she threw it for him to chase.

Which of us was the ghost? I wondered again. Because that place was real; I could touch it, I could smell it – the moist, green smell of grass, the damp, spicy scent of rotting leaves, the faint, sulphurous tang that hung in the air, and Bruno's warm, doggy odour that made me think of my gran's house.

And over on my left, I could see the cedar, and the long slope of lawn with its flower-beds and monkey puzzle tree and little low hedges and ornamental grasses. I could even pick out the stone seat under its arch of leaves, and beyond it, the house with its delicate conservatory and ivied walls and all its funny castle-tops.

Trails of smoke from the chimneys smudged the misty grey sky. The sun was a pale, watery yellow, and my skin felt cold and slightly clammy. I found myself wishing I was wearing a jumper. Then I pulled myself together and reminded myself of why I was there.

I turned her round to face me. "Lettie," I said firmly. "You did *not* kill your mother. And it really doesn't matter if you read your father's books. You are not wicked, and there's no such place as hell."

She seemed to jump at the last word. Then she stared at me dumbly. At last, she fumbled inside her cloak and took out a small silver locket.

"Papa once gave me this," she said. "I never share her with people, but you are my special friend. You see?" She showed me a portrait of a pretty young woman. "She was beautiful, my mama. It was me who should have died." She sighed. "I have big feet and a huge waist and I freckle in summer."

Her waist looked a lot smaller than mine. I laughed. "Does that mean you shouldn't be alive?"

"Not exactly." She tucked the locket away. "But I shouldn't have hurt her so. You see, Mama was Aunt Harriet's baby sister. Aunt Harriet still carries her handkerchiefs black-edged, in mourning."

I suddenly thought of something. "Was your Aunt Harriet in the room when you were being born?"

"Of course not!" Lettie looked shocked. "She didn't live here then. She came afterwards, to help Papa."

"And Martha?"

"She was my nurse when I was a child."

"So neither of them knew about how you were born." Her eyes widened. "Not even your papa."

She blushed at that. "They say he heard Mama screaming when I was killing her," she said in a low voice.

"Lettie, you didn't kill her," I told her. "It was all lies!"

"*Lies?*" She pronounced the word reluctantly, like a nice girl who's swearing. "The nurse, perhaps, but my aunt's a gentlewoman. English gentlewomen don't," she hesitated, struggling with the word, "tell stories," she finished awkwardly. Then, "Cook did mention once," she muttered, "that poor Mama died of childbed fever…"

"Puerperal fever!" I shouted, pleased that I'd remembered the word. "I know all about that."

"How could you?" She looked at me scornfully. "It's a delicate subject, known only to doctors!"

Then I trotted out all the stuff that Mr

Simms had told us, about germs and antiseptics and clean water supplies, and how these had changed things for women in childbirth.

"How do you *know* all this?" she asked me.

"My teacher told me."

"Has she no modesty?"

"He," I corrected her. "My science teacher's a man."

She stared at me, shocked. "You come from a strange place, demon Jess," she said at last.

"Listen," I told her. "I'm from the future." That bald statement sounded so silly, like something from a sci-fi film. "And we know everything," I claimed stupidly.

"Do you know," she was testing me, "how to tell if someone's a witch?"

That threw me. "We don't believe in witches." Then I took a deep breath. "Some of us don't even believe in God."

"Then how can you tell if you've sinned?"

For the first time, I tried to define what I really believed in.

"I think goodness is a sort of kindness," I said at last, working it out for myself. "Towards other people, and animals and nature. So sinning has got to be the opposite of that." We were approaching the house and by then I was trembling, shivering with cold in my brushed cotton pyjamas. Suddenly I longed for a warm, snuggly duvet.

Was it wishing again?

69

Or was my time there always limited?

Because I never knew what happened, but there I was, in bed.

CHAPTER TWELVE

At school the next day, I just couldn't concentrate.

"Homework, Jess?" Miss Martin asked me pointedly. "When you come down from Planet Nine."

"Left it at home. Sorry," I fibbed. *Lies*, I remembered. Lettie'd clearly thought lying was a serious sin. Yet it hadn't seemed to matter quite so much if a servant did it. So what, I wondered, would she think about me?

Paula walked back with me that day. It was a cold afternoon, but pretty, with lavender clouds spread thinly over a pale blue sky and the first glowing hint that there'd be a spectacular sunset.

"Spring…" She sighed. "Let's go," she suggested, "for a walk in your woods."

My woods? Or Lettie's?

Funny, I thought. Even Paula seemed to

sense that they were private property.

But how I wished they *really* belonged to me.

We took some drinks and some biscuits down as far as the paddling pool. There were no little kids splashing about in it now. It looked like a popped concrete blister (they'd drained it for winter) speckled with thrown-away sweet wrappings and orange peel and rooks squabbling over bits of dry crust.

If there'd been a big lake, I mused, then this might have been its middle, the deepest part...

Somewhere a dog barked hysterically.

I snapped open a can of fizzy drink, then the horror broke around me. It started with that faint, familiar flower smell.

"Can you smell something?" I asked Paula. "Like scent?" Then an icy darkness closed over my head. I struggled to breathe; I was suffocating, drowning.

"Help!" I shrieked.

But Paula coldly said, "No."

"No," she was saying, "I can't smell a thing, apart from your feet!" Then she suddenly stared at me. "Jess, you OK?"

"No, I'm not," I said feebly. "Let's get back to the house."

I clung to her arm as we walked up the path, and for once, I was grateful for the trespassers' entrance.

At home, she poured me a big glass of water

which I couldn't touch. Then she got me to lie down, and rang up her mum to say she'd be late. She stayed around until Ma came back, pestering me with theories. "Bet it was your period," she suggested. "I sometimes feel quite funny just before mine is due."

But the minute Paula left, Ma rang the doctor.

I felt deeply embarrassed. "I'm OK, really!"

"No, you're not," Ma snapped. "I've been watching you for weeks. And either something's bugging you, or you're sickening for the plague!"

Ma always overreacted, but it *did* mean a morning off school.

I didn't try to contact Lettie that night.

There was nothing more she could tell me about the horror.

Maybe our friendship would end now, because I'd got her to believe me, and she could die happy (if anyone ever *could* die happy).

How much longer did she have? I wondered, knowing it would happen before she got to be thirteen. She hadn't looked unwell, but then, what did cholera look like?

Then I thought of something really scary.

Maybe I could catch it.

Maybe that was the evil that lurked around the lake...

73

Next day, Ma took time off and walked me up to the doctor's. It was great missing school because I still hadn't done my homework, and I couldn't come up with yet another excuse.

I leafed through women's magazines and read all the juicy bits. Perhaps, I thought, I should take one back to shock Lettie, but somehow I felt that wouldn't be a good idea.

At last it was our turn.

Dr Roberts looked me over, tapped on my chest and listened to my heart with a stethoscope. Then he spent a long time prodding under my chin and my ears.

"Swollen," he said. "I think you might have a touch of glandular fever."

He took a sample of my blood while I stared fixedly at the freckles on his bald spot. His hair must have been ginger once, like Ma's, I thought, and I wondered if hers would one day turn into that funny goldish grey.

"I'll get you the results in a few days," he told us. "In the meantime, take things easy. Maybe a day or two off school?"

It was nonsense. I didn't even feel unwell.

But then, perhaps, neither had Lettie…

"Can I have a cholera jab?" I asked him.

He looked surprised. "Going somewhere exotic?"

"No, but I've been reading about it and I'm just frightened of getting it."

"No need." He laughed. "Cholera hasn't been around in Europe since the mid-nineteenth century."

We did a little shopping on the way home. Ma kept eyeing me. "You OK?"

"I'm fine," I kept telling her. "Honest. There's nothing wrong with me. I was having an off-day, that's all."

"So why the cholera thing?" she asked again. When Ma thought she was on to something, she just wouldn't let go.

"I already said – we were learning about it at school."

"Then they should have told you," Ma complained, "that you're only at risk in countries where the water is dodgy, instead of filling your heads up with silly ideas!"

She stayed home all afternoon, making calls to the office. "That's all arranged," she told me finally. "I had reports to write up anyway – I can borrow a computer. I'll go in part-time, and get some work done from here."

I pottered around, being bored. I'd be missing choir, I thought irritably. And someone in my class was planning a party.

I yawned over a Tom and Jerry cartoon.

"Try some homework," suggested Ma tartly. "Nothing wrong with your brain!"

I took out a few books. Then I looked up *cholera* in the dictionary. The symptoms were awful – vomiting and diarrhoea and then you died. So it hadn't been around since the mid-nineteenth century – no comfort to me.

That evening, I couldn't eat much, scared I might start throwing it all up. Then I went off to bed with my tummy rumbling. But if I really had cholera, I thought, that blood test would show it. I was tired, just tired; I'd feel better tomorrow…

I read for a while, then switched off the lamp. But I couldn't sleep: I'd been sitting around too much, I'd been worrying. And a full moon came glittering through Stinky Stourby's thin curtains. I could almost have read my book by its light.

I gave up on sleep and tiptoed downstairs, turning on TV softly, so as not to wake up Ma.

I must have passed out on the sofa; I don't know. All I can remember was waking up in a jungle, warm, sweaty, damp, and heavily perfumed with flowers.

CHAPTER THIRTEEN

It wasn't a jungle, I decided.

It was closer to a rainforest…

I'd seen one on a nature programme, and it had looked just like this. There were bright green, feathery ferns winding round each other, big, darker ferns with curled-up tips, and ones like pale seaweed, tangled up with palms and bamboos all struggling for light.

I looked up and saw sunlight between the leaves, then snow crusting the metal spines of a glittering glass roof. Then I looked down and saw plants in *pots* – pink and white geraniums, purple daisies, lilies and small, richly scented orange blossoms with dark glossy leaves. Each plant was even labelled in thin, spidery writing. I felt quite disappointed.

Not even a rainforest, I thought – just a boring old greenhouse, like something you'd find in a garden centre.

"I hoped you would come." Lettie was sitting on a cane chair, with sewing in her lap. "I felt so lonely with only Bruno to talk to. I wanted you to see Papa's winter garden. And I've been thinking of what you told me, about poor Mama."

"You must believe it," I said, forgetting about rainforests. "You really didn't kill her."

Her eyes filled with tears. "You know, no one ever told me that. Not even Papa." She frowned. "But if Martha lied, she *did* teach me how to call up a spirit from the future – with crossed sticks and herbs and the right magic spells."

I grinned. "I don't think the herbs and spells had that much to do with it."

I tried to explain it the way Mr Simms or Ma might have done. "Maybe time gets mixed up sometimes. It's complicated. We had this clever bloke called Einstein, and even he didn't properly understand time. And anyway," I added, "you needed a friend." I put in my bit for Woman Power. "*You* did it," I told her. "*You* called me. You didn't need all that magic stuff. Listen, *you* can change things." I sounded like one of Ma's assertiveness training books. "Tell people about germs," I added pointlessly, even though, for Lettie, it was probably too late.

She sighed. "Who would believe me, even if it's true? I'm just a young girl, with no proper education."

"What does she teach you then, that governess?"

Lettie shrugged. "She sets me tasks. I copy things out of books and learn things by heart. I can tell you the names of all the capital cities in Europe, and I can recite the twenty-third psalm. We do nature study and I am sure I know far more than Miss Hurst," she looked away, "because I read so much in Papa's books. I enjoy drawing flowers, and I can paint in watercolour. I can sew a fine seam and embroider and play the piano. One day, I'll make someone a very good wife – if Aunt Harriet has her way."

She sounded quite scornful, and I didn't know what to say. "What are you making now?" I asked her awkwardly.

She offered me her sampler, and I read the words:

THE GRASS IS GREEN. THE ROSE IS RED
WHERE IS MY WORK WHEN I AM DEAD?

"Creepy!" I shuddered. Then I saw she looked hurt. "Pretty colours," I added lamely. "Will you frame it?"

"I don't know." She flushed. "And truly, I don't care." She paused. "Everyone now is reading Mr Dickens, and we all want to change things, but who listens to women? I feed the poor, with Aunt Harriet; that is our

Christian duty. But one day I would like to do more, much more."

I asked her, "What?"

She was silent for a moment.

"There was a child," she said at last, "who came with his master, last September, to sweep our chimneys. He was six, maybe seven, but he looked like a tiny old man, filthy and covered in sores. And maybe it wasn't the first time he'd had to crawl up inside a chimney, but he was still frightened, weeping, pulling back. Then his master, so my maid told me, forced him to keep climbing by prodding him with a nail on the end of a pole. I wanted to kill that man and so did she." She shook her head. "There are new laws now, but too often they are broken."

"Did you tell your Aunt Harriet?" I asked her. She looked at me incredulously.

"My aunt is a good woman," she said, "but she doesn't like interfering. *Not our place to criticize* is her favourite motto. She believes that God made our stations in life, and that these cannot be changed. God made us fortunate," she explained when she saw my baffled face, "and He made that child poor. So it would be quite wrong, Aunt Harriet thinks, to go against His will. She's quite happy to feed the poor and even clothe them, but nothing more. Educate the labouring classes, she says, and they'll get ideas above their station. But if

I ever inherit," she added fiercely, "I will turn things upside down! And I will never marry, despite Aunt Harriet's plans. I do not wish to die, like my mother died; I have better things to do." She grabbed my shoulders. "Remember, this is a secret," she whispered. "I have told no one but you."

There was a sudden movement behind us. Someone opened a door and a hand gripped my elbow.

"Ow!" I yelled, struggling to get free.

"Miss Laetitia," barked a man's voice. "What would your father say if he saw this gipsy pawing over his plant collection?"

I twisted round and looked up at him. He had dark, floppy hair under an old tweed cap, and dark fuzzy whiskers that stopped just before they got to his chin. He wore an orange cotton scarf and a patched tweed waistcoat and shapeless cord trousers stuffed into heavy boots. Yet he still managed to looked powerful, devious, clever, his eyes shifty and mean, his mouth large, but set in a hard, vicious line.

He started dragging me away. I looked desperately back at Lettie.

"You're boss here!" I yelled. "Tell this yob to let go, or call your Aunt Harriet!"

She dropped her sewing and stared. Then she seemed to make up her mind.

"Josiah Greenwood..." Then her voice faded, and I heard nothing more.

Ma found me in the morning, fast asleep on the sofa.

"What have I told you," she scolded, "about watching late night TV?" She touched me. "You're frozen! I'll make you a hot water bottle. Now for goodness' sake, get back to bed!"

I was thankful to go. My arm was still aching from where that bloke had grabbed me.

But something else was bothering me.

I had seen his face before.

CHAPTER FOURTEEN

Ma woke me up with breakfast.

Breakfast in bed! She hadn't done that since I'd had my bad flu.

"I'm going in to see a client I can't put off," she told me. "I'll be back by lunchtime. Someone's giving me a lift, to help with the computer. Now take things easy," she fussed. "And call me if you need me."

"I'm not sick, Ma," I repeated. "Honest. I feel fine."

That wasn't quite true. I still felt tired.

Tired and scared.

What if I'd been stuck in the past when that man was grabbing me? I'd got back very conveniently; supposing I hadn't? Was my time there always fixed, or could I control it? I'd certainly wanted to be out of *that* guy's hands.

And would it work every time, coming back to the present? Waking up and just being me?

And what *was* real, I kept wondering, and what was just a dream? Maybe *this* was the dream – me and Dad and Ma and school, with Stinky Stourby providing the nightmare bits.

And was there some sort of loop, so that bits of Lettie's time could so easily come twisting into mine? Maybe those brick flowers worked like some sort of magnet, but now it was too late to throw them away. Too late, because I was involved with Lettie. Too late, because until now, I'd never really had a best friend.

So why did I have to choose one who was dead?

Suddenly I found myself thinking of my lost little brother, that baby none of us had ever even known. He'd have been three by now, and we'd have been a proper family, not just Dad and Ma and me.

I reached for a tissue and tried to pull myself together. Maybe I was making all that ghosty stuff up. Maybe I *was* under stress – enough difficult things had happened, and I really didn't want to go to yet another school.

Ma believed that everything, in the end, had a natural explanation – even magic and miracles. Depends on your state of mind, she'd say. Maybe I was making up stories to distract myself, so I could forget about the other things.

I got up and had a brief soak in our lukewarm bath. Then I dressed and made myself a cup of tea. I turned up the radio, and jigged around to a rock band, but I still couldn't let go of my other, dream life...

That man's face had been so familiar – the broad nose, those podgy cheeks, the narrow, shifty eyes.

What had Lettie called him? *Josiah Greenwood!*

That must have been the Josiah who'd clipped the yews. Josiah Greenwood – a good name for a gardener. But there was something else about that name, something that bothered me.

I dug out the letter from the Historical Society, and the photocopy from their archives – of all the people who'd once owned Nightingale Court.

First there was Lettie and her mum and dad.

When they all died, the estate had passed to her dad's younger brother, Charles. That must have been the uncle Lettie'd talked about. She'd mentioned an aunt, too – Aunt Harriet, the one who disapproved of education for women. She sounded really stuffy – not much fun for Uncle Charles.

But wait a minute. It said Charles Benton was married to someone called *Maria*. And stuffy Aunt Harriet wasn't even mentioned.

So whatever had happened to her?

Arsenic, I remembered darkly. It had to be a plot.

Had that girl Maria poisoned boring old Aunt Harriet? Then married Lettie's Uncle Charles and taken over the house?

But Uncle Charles died soon after, didn't he? Convenient for Maria. She was a rich widow now, and she didn't waste much time because, look – there she was, married again.

To that creep, *Josiah Greenwood!* Yuk!

Maybe she'd always fancied him.

Maybe she enjoyed being beaten up.

Maybe he'd been her secret lover...

Arsenic, I thought. *Maybe Maria'd poisoned Uncle Charles, too.*

It was all beginning to turn into something quite gruesome.

I put the stuff away and took out some school books, and it was a relief, for once, to wrestle with maths.

Ma turned up, as she'd promised, at half past twelve, struggling downstairs with a briefcase and computer.

"Got something for you," she said, with one of her secretive smiles. "But you're not going to see it until you've eaten a good lunch."

I'd forgotten about my cholera thing, and my tummy already felt empty. I forgot the cholera completely when I smelt Ma's leek soup.

After we'd cleared up, she announced, "Ta-ra! Ta-ra! Now for the big surprise." She opened up her case and took out four sheets of paper. "Got your modern map scaled up at the copy shop," she said. "Maybe now we can find out about that big house."

We fitted the pieces together, then she brought out some tracing paper. Sometimes Ma thought of *everything*. Sometimes I felt specially glad that she was my mum!

By mid-afternoon, I'd traced most of it out. Then we fitted the two maps together, lining up what must have been the only main road.

"Oh, look!" exclaimed Ma. "That lake is where our woods are. So all of our street would have been part of their garden, and the house would have been," she waved her hand vaguely, "somewhere up there."

I was tempted, then, to tell her. It would have been so easy. *Ma, I'm being haunted. That's what's really wrong with me.* But I knew the sorts of things she'd say, and I didn't want to hear them.

Too bad if I'd made it all up, I thought. Having a friend who was a ghost was rather special.

And after all, we'd be moving in a couple of months, and then the whole thing would be over.

Over for me.

Someone else would have to sort out Lettie. Someone else would have to deal with the horror in the woods.

                         *   *   *

Paula came round after school with lots of hot
gossip.

Someone had fallen in a sports class and
gone off in an ambulance. Jake Norris had
made a complete fool of himself. Miss Levin,
people were sure now, had moved in with Mr
Stevens.

"I'd never live with any man," Paula
declared. "I'd be forced into a role model – all
women are."

"It doesn't *have* to be like that," I argued.
"My mum and dad are really good friends."

"Oh, yeah?" sneered Paula. "So he didn't
walk out on you just before Christmas? And
who's got himself a job a hundred miles away,
so you two just have to tag along? What about
your mum's job? And I mean, you'll be leaving next term and I'm going to miss you."

I'd miss her, too, but I couldn't bring myself
to say it. Instead, we bickered and picked on
each other. It was the same old thing, I
thought: around that flat, we all nagged and
fought; outside it, we were fine.

Bad vibes, Dad had said.

Well, if those murders had happened, it
wasn't surprising.

Perhaps traces of evil deeds could hang
around for ages, I thought, polluting the atmosphere, just like lead or acid rain or nuclear
waste.

CHAPTER FIFTEEN

Horses.

I worked it out. They had to be police horses.

But in *Southwood*?

Yet in the middle of the night they woke me up, clip-clopping down the road. Something heavy rattled and jolted. Then I heard voices coming into the house: a man's voice shouting, roaring, fooling around, then a woman's voice, soothing, calming him down.

Dad? I wondered stupidly. Were he and Ma fighting? But Dad didn't usually come round until the end of the week.

I reached for the switch, but there was nothing. Besides, the room seemed to be already lit, light and shadows mottling the flower-sprigged wallpaper. A smoky lamp was standing on a bead-fringed shawl, its pale, moony face doubled in a small swing mirror. There were several dark-framed portraits of solemn-looking people, and even one of those embroidered samplers. It read:

LORD, LOOK UPON A LITTLE CHILD,
BY NATURE SINFUL, RUDE AND WILD.
O LAY THY GRACIOUS HAND ON ME
AND MAKE ME ALL I OUGHT TO BE.

Then I saw a real fire glimmering in a little black grate, washing pink and orange shadows over blue flowered tiles. And in front of it stood something like a big metal cradle, and while I was wondering what it was for, someone whispered, *"Jess,"* and there was Lettie.

Lettie, my best friend with a name like a sneeze.

She was curled up in a chair, wearing a white cotton nightie, her long dark brown hair brushed out and free. Without the flouncy skirts and baby's bonnets, she could have been just a friend from school with whom I was staying the night.

"I *did* it!" She was looking so pleased with herself. "I told him – did you hear me? And he was so surprised, he let you go. That's why I've been punished, given nursery food, confined to my room. Josiah blabbed to Miss Hurst. Then Miss Hurst complained to Aunt Harriet, and Aunt Harriet meekly agreed Josiah was only doing his duty and asked me what I'd been thinking of, letting a gipsy into the house. I got angry then. I told her that one day this might be my house, that perhaps it was mine already, even if I hadn't come of age. I said that one day, I'd do as I liked. She became tearful, cried, *'Oh, your poor papa!'* and said I was cruel and heartless. Then Miss Hurst sent me away to reflect on my sins. They wouldn't even let me have Bruno."

"Why do they hate gipsies so much?" I asked her.

"Gipsies are supposed to steal horses, kidnap babies, but it seems to me they have enough children of their own." Lettie shook her head. "You know, it doesn't count as murder if you kill a gipsy. People think of them as vermin. I know Josiah does."

Somewhere in the house, I heard a man's voice singing raucously, then dissolving into grunts.

"Who's that?" I whispered.

Lettie went pink. "Uncle Charles." She sighed. "He's been drinking again. He's always drinking."

"That must be tough," I said, "on your Aunt Harriet."

"Oh, he doesn't *live* here." Lettie laughed. "He just comes round sometimes," she rolled up her eyes, "to check on that new governess."

"You mean, he and your aunt are divorced?"

"Divorced? Uncle Charles and Aunt Harriet?"

She laughed. "But they aren't even married! Aunt Harriet's his sister-in-law and terribly old, and Uncle Charles is my father's younger brother." She suddenly became solemn. "He's also my guardian until I come of age."

"Some guardian," I sniffed.

"That's what Aunt Harriet thinks, too, but she dare not say it. Perhaps he was different once. I'm sure Papa had not seen him for many years."

An inner door suddenly opened and a face appeared around it. "Beg pardon, miss." The face was plump and flustered under its white frilly cap. "I've come to empty your bath." The eyes caught sight of me; the jaw dropped open. "Oooh!"

"This is my friend," Lettie said firmly. "And Polly, it's a secret."

"But, miss…"

"Just like your new young man."

"Oooh, miss!" The girl's face went scarlet.

"I won't tell," said Lettie, "as long as you don't."

The girl edged past us with her bucket and jug. "I won't, miss. I swear." She glanced at me, terrified. Then she started scooping water out of the cradle-like thing.

"That was blackmail," I joked, after Polly had left.

"What's blackmail?" Lettie asked.

But I didn't explain. Instead, I started showing off. "We've got proper baths," I boasted (although ours didn't amount to much). "With hot and cold water that comes out of taps." I became enthusiastic. "And we really *do* have machines that fly through the air, and carriages that move without horses, and pictures that move, and we can talk to each other across the world. We've got computers and videos…" Oh, there was so much to explain, it left me breathless. "And we don't kill gipsies," I added smugly. "We don't kill *anyone*. Even murderers."

Lettie looked impressed. "You must be so good," she sighed. "You must be like angels."

I suddenly remembered other things – wars, pollution, homelessness, cruelty to kids. I thought of super-bombs and landmines. It was my turn to feel embarrassed.

"No, we're not," I told her. "We've got a lot of clever gadgets that make life easier, but really, we aren't any different from you."

Lettie suddenly grabbed my hands. "I want to ride in a carriage without horses." She sighed. "I want to fly in a train with wings. Demon Jess," she pleaded, "take me with you when you go."

"I'd like to," I said helplessly. "But I can't. I don't know how it works. I can never be quite sure of getting back myself."

She suddenly broke down. "You see, it's awful. I'm frightened. Miss Hurst and Uncle

Charles are already treating my aunt like some kind of housekeeper. She's always run this house so well that we didn't really need one, but the servants still respected her as mistress. But if Papa *is* dead, then Uncle Charles might be in charge, and I don't know what will happen. My aunt's old-fashioned, I know, but she's loyal." She began to sob. "And after Nurse Martha left, she's been like my mama."

I went over and put my arm around her, not knowing what to say. I couldn't even offer her a tissue. *Cholera,* I remembered, *she might be infectious, don't touch her.* But it was too late by then, and I didn't really care.

Lettie calmed down, and was quiet for a while.

Then she came out with that awful question. "What's my future, demon Jess?"

I shook my head, pretending not to understand.

"If you're really from the future," argued Lettie relentlessly, "you can surely tell me mine."

"I'm not a fortune teller," I muttered. "I'm sure your future will be great." I remembered that list from the Historical Society. I knew what would happen and when, not just to Lettie, but to them all. "Do you know," I needed to distract her, "a girl called Maria?"

"No." She frowned. "Not a girl. But I do know a woman. My governess is called Maria.

She's Miss Maria Hurst."

I gasped. Suddenly, it all fitted.

"Then she'll marry your uncle," I told her. It couldn't do any harm for her to know.

"*Marry?*" Lettie looked horrified. "He couldn't do that. They are certainly more than mere acquaintances. They knew each other before my uncle placed her here. He comes to call on her, like this evening." She blushed. "Sometimes they seem to act like people betrothed. But marry? Beneath his station? Not Uncle Charles. *She's a governess!*"

"How would that stop her marrying him?"

"Oh!" Lettie wailed. "You don't understand. But maybe... Horrid Hurst's ambitious enough, likes to dress as a lady." She picked up a bamboo frame like a swinging cage and tied it round her waist with tapes. Then she grabbed a patchwork quilt and draped it round herself. "My *dear* Lady Jessica!" She offered me a limp hand. "I'm Miss Maria Hurst, the illustrious governess who can't even spell, soon to be wed to Mr Charles Benton." She frowned at me suddenly. "But you left no calling card."

"What's a calling card?" I asked when I'd stopped laughing. "And whatever is that thing you're wearing?"

"Aunt Harriet ordered it. It's called a crinoline. See? It holds out my skirts in the fashionable manner. She's already grooming me to attract a good husband." She spun me around. "But I'd sooner marry a sweeper boy!" She suddenly put on a disapproving face. "No one makes social calls without leaving a card." Then she giggled. "Except you." She pointed. "Demon Jess."

We collapsed onto the rug and Lettie's improvised skirt flipped up ridiculously. She untied the bamboo cage and wriggled out of it. Then she stroked my pyjamas.

"I'd prefer to dress like you," she confessed. "But do young ladies in the future wear nothing but *drawers*?"

I tried to steer the conversation back. "Your uncle should be careful," I told her. "Because I think your governess may be dangerous..." My voice petered out. I couldn't tell Lettie what I really thought.

I couldn't be sure myself. It had only been a guess. Maybe her boozy Uncle Charles had died of pneumonia.

I was still thinking about it when I seemed to wake up. It was dark in my room so I reached for the light switch and read, to distract myself, until the sky turned grey. Then, just after dawn, I fell heavily asleep.

CHAPTER SIXTEEN

Dad came round that weekend.

He was looking really happy.

"I've found us a flat," he crowed. "For a minimal rent, not far from the school where I'll be working. It belongs to their old music teacher, the one who's going abroad at the end of next term." He grinned at me. "Jess, you'll love it. It's near the school grounds, next to a workshop complex. You'll see nothing but trees and grass, so you won't have to take risks if you want to watch wildlife!"

"Great," I said dully.

I was feeling tired again, almost unwell. Dr Roberts had prescribed vitamins and things. "But it's a virus," he'd reminded us. "So there's no point in giving you antibiotics. All we can do is try to build up your resistance. Plenty of rest and lots of good food."

We went out to supper that night, with

some old friends from Lewiston and their daughter Sarah, who'd been at school with me. *A gentle outing won't hurt Jess,* Dad had reassured Ma. But I had little appetite and less conversation, and Sarah and I seemed worlds apart now.

We watched a video to cover our lack of communication, but when Ma came into Sarah's room, she found me half asleep.

Dad rang for a cab.

Then we said *Good night,* and *Thank you,* and *We must do this more often,* and *What a shame it would be if the two girls lost touch.*

On the way home, I closed my eyes again.

"She's not well, I *told* you," muttered Ma.

"Thought it might do her good," growled Dad, "seeing old friends."

They were squabbling quite fiercely as we drew near the flat.

I suddenly took control. "I'll get much worse if you keep going on like this," I told them. "So stop it, both of you!"

And to my amazement, they did.

Paula and her dad dropped by late on Sunday.

"Coming to school tomorrow?" Paula asked.

"No, she isn't," answered Ma.

"Stop speaking *for* me!" I shouted. "You're always doing it and I can't stand it. I'm a lot better," I said to Paula, feeling quite exhausted. "See you tomorrow in History at half-past nine."

After that there was an awkward silence. Dad and Ma clearly didn't feel comfortable with Paula's dad, and I didn't think Paula's dad thought that much of them.

And I longed to sit quietly and talk to my best friend. Lettie... Better make the most of that, I thought, because in a couple of months I wouldn't even *be* there.

We parted quite frostily. I had even squabbled with Paula. We just couldn't help it. There was an atmosphere around us I couldn't define – something invisible and yet it was there, like one of those winds I'd read about that drives people crazy, makes them quarrel and fight. Bad vibes I already knew about, but it was stronger than that, as if whatever had set them off was winding up to a climax.

I went out to the garden for some fresh air and quiet.

"Not those woods!" Ma nagged. "And for heaven's sake, put on a jacket. You know how cold it is out there."

I did, but it didn't seem important now.

I walked down to the fence and looked up at the trees, at their branches smudged like charcoal against the early evening sky. February. Spring. But spring was a cruel season, I found myself thinking. I didn't know why – I'd always liked it before. Perhaps it was the sight of those few garden snowdrops, like small, waxy grave flowers scattered over their tomb of dark winter earth.

Suddenly that bird began singing again, and all at once, I knew Lettie wouldn't live to see Easter.

I began to cry then, silently, tears running down my cheeks. Then a warm arm slid around me, and that Ma-smell was nicer than all the perfumes in the world.

"Come on, love," she said, squeezing me. "Let's get you into bed. For a run-down girl, you've done enough for one weekend."

I gave up and let her baby me, snuggling gratefully under my duvet while she plumped up pillows and even dug out my book from the middle of a heap of junk.

A bit of me still wanted to nark, "Stop fussing, Ma!" But this time, I didn't let myself say it. If we started resisting those bad vibes, I thought, maybe they'd just go away.

Dad came in later with soup and some toast.

"How's my best girl?" he asked. And he looked so contrite, I had to give him a hug.

Happy families, I thought warmly after he'd left. Something poor Lettie would never have known...

The doorbell suddenly rang.

I heard people arguing, Dad shouting, "Totally unreasonable! Our daughter's ill in bed. Call my wife tomorrow and make an appointment."

Then I heard Ma cooing, "Well, if it really won't take long..." I could still hear Dad grumbling and crashing about, and growling things about harassment and uncivilized behaviour.

After a few minutes, Ma came tiptoeing into my room. "Mr Stourby's here, with the building surveyor," she whispered. "They need to make some measurements. It won't take very long."

A tall, nervous-looking man appeared behind her. He glanced across at me, clearly embarrassed. "Sorry about this," he muttered, holding his sonic tape against a wall and recording some figures.

Then Stinky Stourby came in and began walking about and discussing things as if I wasn't even there.

I hadn't seen Stinky Stourby since the day we signed the lease. Now I lay and watched him through half-closed eyes, pretending to be much sicker than I was.

He was wearing casual clothes this time, and they did nothing to improve him – a cap, a heavy beige jacket and a diamond patterned wool shirt in liver-red and green. His thin hair was slicked back, and across his broad nose he wore small, steel-rimmed spectacles. His hands were thick and fleshy, his nails surprisingly jagged and rimmed with black, almost as if he'd been using them to dig up earth.

I'd seen hands like that recently. *Where?*

I closed my eyes and conjured up the perfume of exotic flowers, winter sun dazzling, like a big star, through lacy ferns, Lettie standing next to me with her sewing, then a hand closing round my arm, stubby, dirt-rimmed fingers digging painfully into my flesh, *"Gipsy! Dirty gipsy!"*

I opened my eyes then and stared at Stinky Stourby. The hair was lank and the side-whiskers had gone.

But I was still looking into the face of Josiah Greenwood!

CHAPTER SEVENTEEN

The resemblance was uncanny.

Nightmarish. I grimaced. One Stinky Stourby was more than enough for me.

When he and his sidekick had left, I got out of bed and rifled through my junk for that list of people who'd owned Nightingale Court. But I didn't really need to check, because I already knew it by heart.

After boozy Uncle Charles had come Josiah Greenwood and Maria Hurst, the governess. And they'd had a daughter, Hannah. But had Hannah married? The list didn't say.

Maybe Hannah had married someone called Stourby; perhaps *our* bloke was the great-great-something or other – there had to be a reason why Stourby owned two of the houses in our street. Perhaps his wealth came from family money, not just from the City. It was too much of a coincidence – that family likeness to the fortune-seeking gardener of Nightingale Court.

Fortune-seeking? But wasn't I guessing again?

I picked up my brick flowers (magic? magnets?) and tried to contact Lettie. There was so much I wanted to ask her, tell her, *warn* her – to boil the water, for instance, before she drank it. It didn't seem fair to have to die when you were only twelve.

Then I suddenly thought of something quite shocking.

Maybe it hadn't been cholera.

If her dad had made his brother Lettie's guardian, maybe *he* was next in line, after Lettie, to inherit the house. Then she'd be in the way. Nothing easier, I thought with growing horror, for a big boozy bully like Uncle Charles to kill her. And nothing easier, at that time, to fake the evidence. No DNA testing then, no clever forensic stuff.

How I wished I could rescue her, take her with me.

At least I could warn her.

Lettie, I called. *Laetitia, Laetitia, I'm getting a cold!* And if I hung on tightly to some bit of her, I wondered, could I pull her with me through time? *"Lettie,"* I whispered urgently. *"It's demon Jess."*

And something responded, called out to me.

I went into the back room. Dad was just

104

leaving, giving Ma a goodbye kiss.

It was a kiss that seemed to go on for ever. I unlocked the french windows but they still hadn't moved.

A low mist was rising from the lawns behind me and the few dim lights in the big house were just a speckled haze. And a faint, sickly flower scent filled my throat and nostrils.

"Gipsy!" someone snarled. There was a rustle of skirts, then I saw Maria Hurst quite clearly, her small pink mouth distorted, her eyes luminous and cold and fixed upon me. "We've already warned you!" she spat, but I still couldn't move. She was all sparkle and prettiness. I kept seeing the little bead flowers on the edge of her cape, the glint of spectacles dangling from a velvet ribbon, the glossy oval brooch at her throat and the black lace edging on the flounces of her skirts. I saw those dark, romantic ringlets under her white ribboned cap as she lunged at me and grabbed.

Then I ducked, and ran blindly, plunging round the curve of the lake and into the woods. I thought she'd come after me, but she didn't. I could still see her, standing at the edge of the water, her strange, triangular shape rising out of the mist and reeds. Flowers. *Violets?* The smell seemed to cling to my clothes like a sort of sweet, stale breath.

For safety, I moved further into the woods. It was twilight now, almost dark, and my feet were scratched and already numb with cold. I thought of my duvet, expecting magic – hadn't it happened before? I thought of Ma and Dad kissing, back there in no-time, I even thought of Stinky Stourby in his horrible shirt. I tried calling for Lettie, but nothing changed. Then a bird began singing. In my woods? In her woods?

A bird singing at night... *Nightingale?* Could that be why the house was called Nightingale Court?

A small flurry of wings, and the warbling stopped. Then I heard it repeated in the depths of the trees. I stumbled after it – perhaps it was an omen – but my feet scraped on ridges of icy mud. Dark, it was misty dark, grey brown, all edges blurred, no paths, no way, even if I'd had some idea of where I was going. Suddenly something snapped tight around my ankle, something metallic, like a heavy handcuff.

I tried to undo it but I couldn't. I struggled and stamped but it bit further into my skin. Then I lost my balance and collapsed into bracken and dead leaves. I began to cry. My ankle hurt and I was frightened: this time there seemed to be no way back. I could already see myself as some kind of outcast in the nineteenth century, going on about things that no one understood. Even Lettie might eventually assume I was crazy. *You said you came from the future? Then prove it,* she might say.

A lone goose honked overhead, then I heard the muffled *splash!* as it landed on the lake. A small night bird whimpered and fluttered in its nest, an owl called out mournfully, then that bird began singing again. Something scuttled through the bushes, something squawked, then something scampered. My night eyes spotted a rabbit, but I was long past caring. My fingers hurt with the cold and I couldn't stop shivering.

Then I became aware of something large moving stealthily, snapping twigs and rustling ferns. I made myself stop crying and held my breath, but the chattering of my teeth, I was sure, would give me away. There was a sudden *twang!* The rabbit squealed once, then was silent. A hand came out and released it, dragging it away. Then a head came through the bracken.

"Brute's caught a gipsy girl," someone muttered. I drew back as his hands fiddled with the thing on my ankle. All at once, it clicked open and I was free, but I couldn't run, couldn't move and my leg was still hurting. "In this weather..." He sounded angry. "Could have died of cold. That rat ought to swing for it. You don't set traps to catch your own kind." Rough hands helped me up. "Can you still walk?"

I nodded.

"I'll take you to my mother," he whispered.

"She don't live far. She'll check you over: she's got good herbs and poultices. Rest over until you feel better. Then you can get back to your own people."

Oh, if only I could, I thought silently.

"You're shivering." He took off his jacket and draped it around me and I looked down and saw the dead rabbit's ears. He grinned at me. "He'll make a right good stew, that one."

Not for me. I shuddered and tried not to notice that soft, warm weight against my arm.

We made our way through the woods, ducking sometimes, stopping and starting, moving cautiously, never once speaking. He found a gap in the fence, pushed me through, then followed me. I watched as he carefully replaced two iron railings, pushing them into the ground, then piling up leaves around their base.

"Always cover your tracks," he whispered. "But then, being a gipsy you'd know all about that."

We trudged across a meadow, walking through swirls of mist. I clung to his arm.

"That devil, Greenwood," he growled. "I'd like to see him caught in one of his own traps – I'd leave him there to rot. And that poor young lady's father could join him for all I'd care. Thick as thieves, those two. Master and servant, not right, against nature, though it's not my place to say it. All they seem to care about are the master's fancy plants. Mr Benton's been training him to caretake – he's always going off on them experditions. You ever see into that greenhouse of his?"

When I said *Yes,* he grinned. "Well, you shouldn't have and lived! What were you up to – robbing the place? Not that I'd care. That Benton guv'nor cares more about his fancy rhodiedundrums," he stumbled over the word, "than his own flesh and blood. And she's such a sweet young lady, that Miss Laetitia. Ain't natural, I say."

I needed to know more. "What about his brother? He seems to care about *him.*"

He stopped and stared at me. I could see him a bit more clearly now, and he wasn't much older than me. His hair looked damp under a flat wool cap and his face seemed friendly.

"You know a lot about the big house for a gipsy," he said.

"I'm not a…" I quickly made up a suitable story. "I'm part of the family, a poor relation. I'd tell you more…" I pretended to fall.

Then he caught me and carried me the rest of the way.

CHAPTER EIGHTEEN

The cottage smelled, but the woman was kind.

She made me lie down on a prickly mattress. Then she bathed my sore leg with a piece of rag, and dripped something sticky into my cuts. "Good honey," she explained proudly. "From our own hives."

When she lifted the lid of a pot simmering next to the fire, the room suddenly filled with a heavy smell of soup.

"Better take some nourishment after all that cold," she said, ladling me a bowlful. But I couldn't touch it.

I caught a glimpse of the rabbit, slumped over the table like a piece of bloodied fur, and began to feel sick.

The woman began singing:

*"Pay attention, you poachers, wherever you
  may be,*

Can you answer my question and tell unto
me,
Who owns the wild hare that runs over the
lea?"

"S-s-sh," I heard the boy say. "Girl says she's kin to them up at the big house."

"Nonsense!" His mother slapped her thighs and laughed. "She's a gipsy. Look at them beads and braids, and that dark skin." Her voice dropped. "Or maybe she be some kind of fallen woman – out there in the cold, wearing nothing but a shift and drawers. But quality she ain't." She sighed. "Not for me to pass judgement, though. She be human, same as us."

Thanks for nothing, I thought.

I closed my eyes. I felt exhausted...

"Jess!" Someone was scolding me. "You're asleep in your chair."

I looked up and saw my wonderful dad. *I'd come back! I'd come back!*

"What's wrong with your bed?" he teased me. "Got fleas?" He shook out the duvet and plumped up the pillows. "Now get in there," he ordered, giving me a kiss.

After he'd gone, I checked on my ankle. It still ached, but there wasn't a mark on it. I tried to puzzle it out, but I was really very tired, and my bed was soft and warm and smelt of clean laundry, and my room didn't

111

pong of smoke, soup and sweat.

I glanced at the brick flowers, still lying on my shelf. Then I switched off the light and drifted sweetly into sleep, grateful that the magic – or whatever it was – had still worked. Yet when I woke up next morning, I did not feel rested. A grey, cold light came filtering through my curtains, and I looked out into the drab tones of a sunless February day.

Ma tiptoed into my room with a breakfast tray.

"I'm getting up," I told her brusquely.

She looked instantly hurt. "You might say thank you."

I felt irritated, cross. "Stop fussing over me," I said. "I'm not ill."

Ma stamped out. I heard her slamming down the tray and rattling the dishes. I dressed, went into the kitchen and sat down at the table, feeling awful.

Why on earth had I been so rude?

"Sorry, Ma," I said, but it didn't seem to work.

"Post for you." She slapped down a large, fat envelope. Then she switched on her computer and cut me off.

I tore open the package. It was full of photocopied pages from some ancient newspaper. At first I was puzzled. Then I read the letter. It was from that nice librarian who'd helped me with the maps.

Dear Jessica,

I thought you might like to include a few sample pages from early local newspapers (photocopies, of course!) to enliven your school project – or am I too late? You see, your enthusiasm was so infectious that I joined the Historical Society myself!

These pages date from 1851 – the year of the Great Exhibition, very exciting stuff!

The Society makes school visits, holds workshops, and would be pleased to give your school any support it needs with its local history project. Do let me know how you get on.

All the best,

Sue Brown

1851 – the year of that Great Exhibition.

1851 – the year that Lettie died.

I started leafing through the pages, gawping at ads for dodgy-sounding pills and painful-looking corsets. There was a piece about the Exhibition, opening in May.

There'd been a gruesome murder in Parsonage Lane, and a fight in a pub. Work was completed on another grand new railway station, and it would shortly be opened by his Worship the Mayor.

Then I saw it:

GENTLEMAN BOTANIST'S DAUGHTER
DROWNED IN TRAGIC ACCIDENT

THE BODY OF MISS LAETITIA BENTON, ONLY CHILD OF WILLIAM BENTON AND CATHERINE BENTON (DECEASED) HAS BEEN RECOVERED FROM A PARTLY FROZEN LAKE AT NIGHTINGALE COURT, SOUTHWOOD.

THE ACCIDENT TOOK PLACE ON FEBRUARY 25TH. MISS BENTON WAS APPARENTLY ATTEMPTING TO RESCUE HER DOG, BRUNO, WHO WAS STRANDED ON THE ICE. HEROIC RESCUE EFFORTS ON THE PART OF HER GOVERNESS, MISS MARIA HURST, AND THE HEAD GARDENER, JOSIAH GREENWOOD, WERE TRAGICALLY IN VAIN.

RELATIVES HAVE SO FAR BEEN UNABLE TO CONTACT MR WILLIAM BENTON, WHO IS AT PRESENT TRAVELLING IN NEPAL. FUNERAL ARRANGEMENTS, THEREFORE, REMAIN IN THE HANDS OF MR CHARLES BENTON, THE UNFORTUNATE YOUNG LADY'S UNCLE AND GUARDIAN, WHOSE GRIEF IS INEXPRESSIBLE.

I bet it was, I thought.

Had grieving Uncle Charles arrived for a bit of hanky-panky with the governess and found his niece conveniently in danger on the ice? Had the governess done it? Maybe they'd been working together. I could easily imagine that little procession across the ice, hear the terrified dog howling, see the slender, black-gloved hand place itself firmly on Lettie's back. Or had it been Josiah who'd pushed her in?

Then I noticed the date on my letter. February 24th. Posted yesterday.

So today was Lettie's death day, a day when evil had triumphed so completely that it reached out and tainted things centuries later.

Murder. It had to be.

But why pick on us? Why on me?

Perhaps because I was the same age as her, I reasoned. Maybe no twelve-year-old girl had lived here since Lettie died.

And all day long I kept imagining I heard it – Lettie's plaintive voice calling for help. And all day long I kept feeling chilly, even with an extra jumper, and leggings under my jeans. I kept seeing those icy waters closing over her head, closing over my own head...

Because I was her friend, and I'd done nothing to stop it.

What could I do?

What could I have done?

If you change even a small thing in the past, Mr Simms had said, *you could change your whole future. You might even cease to exist. That's why time travel isn't really possible.*

And after yesterday's experience, I never wanted to go back. I'd even resolved to throw away the brick flowers. It was dustbin day tomorrow, and they could go off with the rubbish.

But I couldn't bring myself to do it.

Lettie was my friend. I wanted to see her again.

Just once, that was all.

I needed to say a proper goodbye.

By lunchtime, Ma'd applied the psychology and turned apologetic.

"I shouldn't have jumped on you like that," she said. "You're not yourself; you're not well."

"Oh, stop being a doormat," I told her. "I shouldn't have been so rude. I did try to say sorry."

"I know, love." She gave me a hug and it was all over.

I watched cartoons on TV and picked at some schoolwork. I turned on the radio and tuned in to a quiz show. Then I put on a tape and listened to my favourite group.

Paula turned up at half-past four with a big bag of grapes. "For the sick," she announced dramatically.

"Thanks a lot," I said feebly.

She was settling down for a gossip when I looked desperately at Ma, and Ma took over.

"Ten minutes only," she told Paula. "Jess is still very tired and has to rest."

"Thanks, Ma," I said afterwards. "I just

116

couldn't face it. I think I'll flop on my bed and finish my book."

I went up to my room and closed the door.

Then I picked up the brick flowers and willed Lettie to call me.

CHAPTER NINETEEN

I dozed over my book, only half reading it. I didn't even bother to switch on the lamp.

Downstairs, Ma turned on the radio and I heard the distant jabber of the News.

I closed my eyes for a while, and then I opened them.

Yes...

I am in a dimly lit room full of books, like a library. It smells of polish and candlewax.

The tops of the bookshelves have borders of carved wooden leaves, and even the fireplace has big sculpted patterns that remind me of something in a church. There are plant prints, a draped bust of a grim-looking bloke on a yellow marble pillar, a framed portrait of a smiling woman and a pale wreath of dried flowers under a small glass dome.

One of those books lies open on a desk. I go

up to it and flick through its gold-edged pages. *The Voyage of the Beagle*, it's called – sounds like a script for a Disney film, but the pages are thin and the print is too small and there are only small, black and white pictures.

I suddenly hear a sob. I turn and see Lettie slumped between the open doors of the conservatory, her skirts all spread out, her shoulders hunched and shaking.

"Lettie," I whisper, but she doesn't reply. *"Laetitia, Laetitia,"* I say. *"I'm getting a cold!"*

She looks round then. "Oh, Jess!" She struggles up and puts her arms round me. "Bruno's missing," she tells me. "He's been gone for hours. And it's cold out there – look."

I look. The glass roof of the conservatory is shrouded with snow and I could see nothing out of the windows.

"Fog, too," wails Lettie. "We've searched and we've searched. And I think Josiah's put down traps for poachers and gipsies and if Bruno's caught in one, he'll die of cold."

At that moment the door's flung open, and I duck back rapidly behind the big palms.

I hear a middle-aged woman's voice. "You wilful girl! What are you doing in your father's study?"

"Reading." Lettie sounds defiant, but still weepy. Then, "Have they found Bruno, Aunt Harriet?"

"You're lucky." There's a rustle of fabric, a sweep of skirts. "Miss Hurst has found him.

She says he's stranded on the ice in the middle of the lake – he must have been after a goose. Josiah has gone for a rope and a plank, but that animal won't move unless you call him."

"I'll go," cries Lettie. "I'll go at once!" And my heart sinks. I *have* to stop her!

"Put on your wrap and your gloves," fusses Aunt Harriet. "It's foggy out there, and the snow is still thick on the ground."

Lettie follows her out. I can't do a thing; she's forgotten all about me.

I wait for a moment, then I run across the room and through the hall, past a pop-eyed maid and a glowering tiger head and a big glass-fronted cupboard full of stuffed birds.

I belt down the steps and into the garden and find myself wading through a foot of snow. The fog is like sheets of pale yellow tissue paper. I can just make out the silhouette of Lettie plunging down the slope, and not far ahead of me, what must be Aunt Harriet, her skirts dragging a trail through the blanket of white.

I circle round her, then at last catch up with Lettie.

"Don't go down there!" I yell. "They're going to *kill* you. I *know*."

But she glances at me coldly, as if I am crazy. "Bruno's out there," is all she can say.

I make a grab for her then. "Lettie, please listen." But she pulls herself away and goes on running.

I lose her in the fog.

Then I lose myself. I can still hear voices – strangely clear in that awful, wrapped-up silence. *"Over here!"* a woman's calling. *"Careful on the ice, miss…"* That's a man. I hear a dog howling, then Lettie calling frantically, *"Bruno! Bruno! Here! Over here!"*

Stiff reeds and rushes pierce the snow, and I put out my foot and step onto ice. Moving forward cautiously, testing the surface, I try to steer myself towards the sound of Bruno barking. I've suddenly had this mad idea – what if I rescue him myself? I see myself walking towards them, holding up Bruno, Lettie smiling ecstatically, Miss Hurst glowering, defeated.

But there would still be time for them to steer Lettie murderously onto thin ice because I couldn't possibly rescue Bruno in time.

It's going to happen, I remind myself. *It's already happened. I can't save her. There's nothing more I can do.*

I slither through more spears of frozen reeds, then suddenly plunge into thick, soft snow again. At first I'm puzzled. Then I realize what's happened. I've lost my way, come across the narrowest point of the lake. I stumble past snow-covered brambles, then see the dark trunks of trees.

Woods. I'm defeated. I'm back in the woods.

But the barking seems closer now, not out on the lake, but somewhere quite near. I think

I spot something moving and I trudge towards it. Then I see him, tied up to a tree with a short length of rope.

Change a bit of the past, Mr Simms had told us, *and you might cease to exist.* But I don't care, I don't care.

"Brun-o!" drift the voices from the other side, and he whines and wriggles and barks and whimpers.

Those rats lied to her! I thought. They set it up – the governess and Josiah. The fog and the ice were all that they needed.

I work frantically. (I think – maybe the uncle's paying them.) My fingers are numb and Bruno keeps licking them and anyway, I was never any good with knots.

The rope at last begins to loosen, the dog wriggles free. Then he runs off into the fog.

I try running after him, but it's hopeless. There's nothing I can do. I begin to cry – warm, salty tears dribbling into my mouth.

Suddenly I hear a shriek and someone yelling, "Bruno! Bruno!"

There's a scream, people shouting, a dog barking hysterically.

Voices, confusion, a dull splash, more voices…

Then silence. Sudden silence wrapping me, like a soft, dark quilt.

Silence and darkness.

Darkness.

Oblivion.

PART TWO

CHAPTER ONE

I come out of a deep, dark, dreamless sleep, and feel something being slipped from under my armpit.

"Still a bit high." This woman is shaking a thermometer. It's Dr Roberts. She stays freckled, I remember, even in March.

"Rest, rest and more rest," she's saying. "That's the only effective treatment for glandular fever."

I look at her sleek, coppery-grey hair. She must have been a proper redhead once, like Ma, I think. Maybe one day Ma's hair will go that colour.

Murphy suddenly jumps onto my bed and starts pawing at the cushions. I reach out to stroke him, but already something's feeling not quite right.

I find myself announcing primly, "But we're not allowed cats."

Ma seems astonished. "Since when, Jess Jenkins?"

I sleep again and wake, and sleep and wake. Dad comes in, plays music, tells me silly jokes. Sometimes this little kid curls up on me. He's funny. I like him.

Greg. My little brother.

My little *brother*?

"When did we have him?" I ask.

Then Ma sighs. "Oh, Jess, not *again*."

I've been pestering her, as if asking for proof. "Show me," I keep saying. So she brings out the album and I can't disagree. I mean, there we all are – me, my dad and Ma with our new baby. Gregory, we'd called him, to please my Irish gran. Then Joseph (well, what else?) to please my dad.

Photos feed your memory. I now remember Ma being enormous and me being embarrassed – well, I was still in Juniors and some of the kids in my class were really mean.

I remember Gran coming down to help, and Dad taking Ma to hospital, and the first time I saw my brother, just like one of those troll dolls, all red-faced and hairy and unbelievably small.

I flip forward through the album and watch him changing, growing, turning himself into our funny, small Greg. I see pictures of his last birthday party. A riot, Ma reminds me. A flat full of three year olds? Well, it would be, wouldn't it?

"But where did he *come* from?" I ask like a kid. Ma looks concerned, but Dad just winks and grins.

"Same place as you," he tells me. "Under a gooseberry bush."

"Oh, Dad!" I protest. Then I start giggling, and just can't stop.

I'm getting better, stronger.

"We do seem to be winning," says Dr Roberts. I'm admiring her amber earrings; I want some like that.

I've been downstairs, watched TV, played briefly with Greggie. Friends drop by with school news. Not my best friend – she's been away and I'm really missing her.

Paula Thomson came yesterday. She's OK, but she never stops talking. Ma's really tough; didn't let her stay for more than ten minutes.

I wish I could go back to school.

After Easter, says Dr Roberts.

After your birthday, points out Ma.

Thirteen, I'll be thirteen, an unlucky number…

It's funny how sometimes nothing feels real. I can't explain it. I still find myself pestering Ma, asking things about Greg. I even look at Murphy as if he's a ghost-cat.

Dreams.

Memories? But whose? Not mine.

But I just know there's something I've got to work through.

One afternoon, I go to bed with a book, but I can't read it. The March sun's so dazzling I have to close my eyes.

Ma comes in and finds me half asleep. She picks up the book from the floor.

"More shut-eye for you, my girl," she says, pulling down the blinds, but that cool spring light still comes sneaking round the edges.

I turn and see my face in the bedroom mirror. I think I look awful, all moony-eyed and pasty, and those strange thoughts start fluttering again, like moths, inside my head.

I ignore them, try imagining myself with chunky amber earrings, but all I can see is the spot on my chin. Then I stare at my reflection. That *is* me.

Isn't it?

What's real? I keep asking. What's real?

I give up on that one. Perhaps I'm going nuts.

I lie back against the pillows and focus on the jokey GET WELL cards and the pots of daffodils and freesias people in my class have sent me.

Downstairs, Ma's switched on Playschool. I can hear Greggie singing some nursery rhyme.

I'm feeling sleepy again. I close my eyes, and

try to pin down those fluttering memories, those shadowy images that keep coming into my head. I seem to see them flitting round the flower bricks in our ancient garden wall.

I concentrate. Something tells me this time I've got to remember. I snatch at one of those images and this time I hold it.

Autumn, it's autumn…

CHAPTER TWO

I wake up slowly, trying to hang on to some long, elaborate dream, some confused nonsense about whether I'm actually me and if I've really got a little brother.

There is something heavy, warm and wriggly in the crook of my knees.

"Read me a story?"

I sigh. You bet I've got a little brother.

"Stop pestering your sister!" That's Ma.

"Greg's OK." I yawn. "He's not bothering me."

I drift off again, still trying to pick up the threads. Funny thing about dreams – they're so real when you're having them, but when you wake up, you just forget. And even if you remember, they turn out to be rubbish.

I stop trying – why bother?

Straightaway I feel light, free, *new*.

Amazing, I think. Well, perhaps it was a

nightmare. Except it's late afternoon. A *day-mare*, then...

I wake up properly now, wriggle sideways on to my elbow.

Greg snuggles up to me. "Want the sleepy bear book."

I groan and start reading. How many more times? "OK." I'm resigned. "'Once there were two bears. Big Bear and Little Bear...'" I know the words by heart now, and so does he.

We finish the book. Then Ma plucks him off me. I get a wet, slobbery kiss. "Bye-bye, Big Jess."

And I say, "Bye-bye, Little Piggie," like I always do.

After he's gone, I go over and pull up the blind. My fingers itch for my prize camera. It's pretty out there: what have I been missing? Late afternoon sunlight's picking out all the pinks, oranges and mauves of our newly planted primulas, and drawing slanting gold patterns through the spidery shadows of trees. I watch next door's cat slouch menacingly across the lawn, scramble up the brick wall of our communal gardens, crouch, freeze, then drop over into the woods. *Some mouse has bought it,* I think cynically.

I see Greggie running to join some toddlers in the sandpit. Then a crash and a bang tells me Dad's come home, with what sounds like half my class. He pops his head round the door.

"How's my best girl?"

"Fine," I tell him. "Great." It's true. I feel terrific. Maybe daymares are the answer to glandular fever; maybe someone should do some more research. "I slept," I say, "for ages."

He shrugs. "Guess you needed to."

Friends look in on me briefly, crowding round his back.

"Hi, Jess. Get better!"

"Snap out of it, Jess Jenkins. Class Two needs you!"

"Can't have Southwood School Pageant without Jellyroll Jess!" That's Stephen Stourby.

"Shut your face!" I tell him (funny thing is, I really fancy that boy).

They go outside. I hear their voices receding down the garden, and I watch them from the window arranging themselves round Dad and his guitar as if he's some kind of black Pied Piper.

I can hear that nervous, antique jazzy stuff he's playing, see the group posing stiffly, squabbling about correct places, then beginning to dance, jerking their elbows like chickens and waggling their knees. The Charleston – what a joke! *Doo-doo-dee-doo-doo*. "Southwood in the Twenties", that's supposed to be.

132

I put on my dressing-gown and shuffle downstairs. I'm hungry, ravenous. And my head feels quite clear now, as if a whole lot of bad stuff has been swept away.

Swept away, slept away.

Slept away, dreamt away.

It's as if I know who I am for the first time in weeks.

Ma brings me soup and toast and a piece of apple tart. Then she trots outside to pick up Greg. She's lost weight, been exercising, playing tennis. She's so happy these days – I can feel it, I can see it. She loves driving our old banger, and she practically runs that child guidance clinic. And kids get sorted, even if her stuff doesn't always work on me. We fight. So what? It's never serious. It's just that we're different, Ma and me.

Paula Thomson ought to talk to her – maybe *she'd* get sorted. She had such a hang-up about her parents' divorce, but she says she's now working on her relationship with her dad. Whatever that means. Paula's always into something deeply psychological. Her latest fad seems to be Radical Feminism – wonder what that dad of hers makes of that?

"Guess, what? Cath's here," announces Ma, and my middle feels warm because Cath's my best friend. "And she's got a surprise for you. Close your eyes."

I close them and wait.

There's a shuffle and a rustle and a giggle and a snort. Then, "You can look now."

I look.

She's wearing this old-fashioned blue dress with an enormous skirt, and long-legged white knickers that stick out below the hem. She's put on ballet shoes over thick white socks, and a grey bonnet tied with ribbons over a frilly white cap.

"Lettie!" I gasp (I've no idea why).

"S-s-sh." Cath lays a finger on her lips. "Don't embarrass me," she says. "You're the only one who knows I've got a third name. But you're right." She starts marching stiffly up and down. "I'm my great-great-great-grannie who started that Ragged School. Remember?" She pulls a posh face. "Miss Laetitia Benton." Then she grins. *"Laetitia, Laetitia..."*

"I'm getting a cold!" we both shriek.

I suddenly shiver. Funny how sometimes you feel you've played a scene before...

She twirls round for me to admire her costume. "Mum made most of it," she admits. "But the knickers are real." She hoiks up the cage that holds out her skirts and I spot her navy M&S briefs through the opening in the cotton. I realize then that those modest long drawers are just two tubes of fabric tied at the waist!

Not much point, really, if they don't cover

the naughty bits!

Cath picks up what I'm thinking, giggles, splutters, "Split crotch! Split crotch! Rude, rude!" She lets go of the cage thing and her skirts swing like a pendulum. "This crinoline's real, too," she says, "although Mum had to fix the horse-hair bits and tapes. Imagine having to wear one! After the Festival, we're donating it to the Historical Society."

She unties the tapes and lets it fall. Then she squats down beside me, her skirts all spread. "*Your* costume's easy," she complains. "Just bare feet and an apron and dirt on your face."

"Oh, yes." I nod. "Stylish! Just what I always wear."

She gives me a hard look. "Swap if you like. I don't mind being an urchin…" She suddenly looks concerned. "I mean, you'll be better by May, Jess? You'll be better in time for your birthday, next week?"

Greg comes stomping out of the kitchen. His face has a milk moustache. Upstairs, Ma's running him a bath.

"See you later!" we call after him.

"Alligator!" he replies.

I turn back to Cath. "I'm better now," I tell her. "Honest. And I'd rather be an urchin – no lines to remember."

The light's fading. Outside it's already chilly. Dad and the others come pouring in, rubbing their hands and slamming the

135

french windows.

They all gawp at the crinoline. "What's that?"

Cath demonstrates.

"Sex-y!" whistles one of the boys.

Then Ma comes down and takes over. "Straight home, the lot of you," she orders, as if they were six. "This girl needs a bit of quiet." And Dad doesn't say a thing!

I'm acutely embarrassed. "Oh, Ma!" She's so *bossy*.

But all the same, I'm glad to see them go. Cath's bursting to talk and I haven't seen her for ages.

Ages?

Feels more like centuries.

CHAPTER THREE

We go up to my room.

Cath's carrying a supermarket bag that's bulging with goodies – books, papers, goodness knows what.

She waits while I pull on pants and a sweater, and attempt to sort out my unwashed hair.

"Try dreadlocks," she suggests, untying her bonnet and pulling off her cap. In that grey-blue dress she looks suddenly quite ghostly, like some prim maiden from the far distant past.

She tips the bag up carefully, arranges stuff across the bed. "We got my gran searching," she tells me, "and a couple of crumbly aunties. We found old letters, postcards, photos – all kinds of things."

The whole project has clearly got under her skin. Well, it got under mine, too, before I became sick. I mean, we're in charge of the mid-nineteenth century. "The Beginning", they're calling it, and it's opening the pageant so it's got to be good.

It was me who first noticed those flower bricks in the garden wall, but it was Cath who started researching her great-great-great-grannie, the woman who once lived in that big house. Laetitia Benton. Great-great-great-gran Laetitia. Sounded frightfully grand. Sounded frightfully posh.

But Cath's family is. Posh, I mean. They *owned* these four big houses until they decided to turn them into a co-op. She's even got three names.

"What's the *L* for?" I wheedled. "You're my best friend, I won't *tell* anyone."

"Laetitia." Cath groaned. "I'm Catherine Sarah *Laetitia*. After my great-great-great-gran. I don't mind the Sarah, but …" she put her finger under her nose, "that name sounds like a sneeze. Listen. *Laetitia, Laetitia, I'm getting a cold!*"

I laughed. "Bet her friends called her Lettie."

But Cath shook her head. "She couldn't have had many. Not till much later. She kept a sort of journal when she was a kid, and she seems to have had a pretend friend she called *Demon J*. Well, you don't make up friends unless you're seriously lonely. You see, her

138

mum died when Laetitia was only a tiny baby and then her dad didn't really want her. Seems she was brought up by this aunt – Aunt Harriet – while her dad was away looking for new kinds of plants. He was an amateur botanist, quite famous; there's a bit about him in a natural history book, and I've got newspaper cuttings – look." She passed over some A4 sheets. "We got the cuttings copied – they're much too fragile to handle. But like this, we can cut them out and make them part of our collage."

I remembered then. "I did some of the Great Exhibition," I told her. "That woman in the library was really nice – I'm sure she didn't charge me enough for all the copying I did. And Paula Thomson told me she's done Queen Victoria."

"We do *not* approve," jokes Cath, looking down her nose.

I glance through the cuttings. There's one that seems to grab me.

TRAGEDY AT NIGHTINGALE COURT

THE BODY OF MISS MARIA HURST, GOVERNESS TO MISS LAETITIA BENTON, HAS BEEN RECENTLY RECOVERED FROM THE LAKE AT NIGHTINGALE COURT. MISS HURST HAD FALLEN THROUGH THIN ICE IN AN ATTEMPT TO RESCUE HER YOUNG CHARGE'S PET DOG. "GREATER LOVE HATH NO MAN THAN THIS."

"That's a bit over the top," sniffs Cath,

reading it with me. "Bet she was just showing off. Bet she did something stupid."

I was surprised at this, coming from Cath.

"That's not very kind," I tell her. There's a photo of the governess. She looks quite young and pretty. "Seems a bit sad," I say.

But Cath still isn't moved. "I know she was supposed to be brave and all that. But there's something about her face that gives me the creeps. Anyway, you want to hear about Laetitia."

"Lettie," I correct her.

"OK, Lettie." She picks up a photo mounted on thick card and I see a solemn-looking girl of about fifteen posing next to a bloke in a top hat.

"She looks a bit like you," I say. "Who's he?"

"That's her dad," Cath explains. "He died soon after that, of some disease he'd picked up on his travels. And serves him right," she added viciously.

"So what happened to her?" I ask. "Did she ever marry?"

Cath gives me a glance of withering scorn. "How do you think *I* happened if she hadn't?" She picks up another photo – a seated bride, all smiley in orange blossom and lace, and the groom standing behind her, looking sort of humble and shy. Funny thing is, he seems vaguely familiar, too…

140

"The great-great-great-gran's quite old in that." Cath counts on her fingers. "Must have been at least thirty. And see these kids?" She picks up another photo. "They're from her Ragged School. Her rotten dad left his *brother* that big house – they didn't think women could deal with property. Then the brother died. He was a boozer. Lettie makes jokes about him in her diaries – I'll show you. And *he* was supposed to be her guardian – I mean, that was a joke! Look, here he is."

I see a blurred, faded image of a small, plump bloke with side whiskers and vague, watery eyes.

"He fell downstairs." Cath giggled. "Bet he was drunk out of his mind. But of course the papers reported that he'd died of pneumonia. He was always going to 'loose women', Lettie says. She even suspected her governess was one – it was Uncle Charles, after all, who'd got her the job. She writes that the governess and her uncle had 'an understanding' – I suppose that must have meant they were sleeping together. So Lettie finally got the house, which she turned into a school for poor kids. She even let a couple of handicapped kids in, which in those days was really daring – people just assumed they were thick. And some of those 'kids' were almost the same age as her. See this bloke?" She pointed. "Son of a tenant farmer and she *married* him! That awful dad

141

of hers must have turned in his grave!"

"They were funny about class," I muse. "A bit like racists."

Cath nods. "Peasants weren't human."

"Some peasants still aren't." I grin. "Like old Grumpy Greenwood. If that bloke could do a mean thing for someone, I bet he'd go out of his way to do it!"

Cath giggles. "You should see what he's done to his hair while you've been sick – dyed it *black* and plastered it over the bald bits on his scalp! Must think it makes him look sexy."

"To what?" I gasp. "A skunk?"

But Cath shakes her head. "He's not all bad, got some virtues. He's a brilliant gardener – seen all those primulas? And Mum would never fire him, although she really can't stand him. You see, his family goes way, way back."

"To that big house?"

She nods.

"You know, you're really our landlords." I've told her that before and it always makes her mad.

It does now. "Oh, shut up! You know we're not. This is a housing co-op: we share things. And my parents couldn't have gone on maintaining all those bedsits. We're not rich, you know."

I sigh. "But your family's special."

"No more than yours," she says.

"But you go way, way back."

"So does everyone, dopey. How do you think you got here?"

I'd never thought of that.

Jamaica – I had a grandad out there, and aunties and uncles. And before that, East Africa – maybe *my* great-great-what's-it was a tribal chief! Then there's Ma – Liverpool, then County Cork, more and more people as I go further back, and all of them getting together just to make me and Greg. Wow – was that impressive!

"Thanks, Lettie," I tell her.

Cath sighs. "Don't start *that* again."

But, "Thanks, Lettie." I need to say it. I don't know why. "How old was Laetitia when she died?" I ask.

"Oh, ancient. In her eighties." Cath shuffles through the mess of papers, then picks up a photo. "Want to see something really creepy?"

I'm looking at a photo of a gravestone. SAMUEL THOMERSON, it says.

"Who's Samuel Thomerson?" I ask.

Cath sighs. "Read the whole thing."

So I do.

SAMUEL THOMERSON. BELOVED SPOUSE OF LAETI-TIA CATHERINE AND FATHER OF CATHERINE HAR-RIET MAY. DEPARTED THIS LIFE JULY 20TH, 1901. MAY HE REST IN PEACE. I go on reading. LAETI-TIA CATHERINE THOMERSON, WIFE OF THE ABOVE. FELL ASLEEP MAY 1ST 1921. "A GOOD

I notice the pink roses in the vase below.

"One of us always takes fresh flowers for them, once a year." Cath shrugs. "It's a family ritual…"

I have an odd feeling that something's come full circle – something to do with a dream that I can't remember.

"Tell you a secret," Cath says suddenly. "I'm going into politics – don't laugh! But so much needs changing and it seems to be a good way to do it. Anyway, it's in my blood. You know, one of Laetitia's daughters was a suffragette, wanted votes for women, even chained herself to the railings of the Houses of Parliament." She looks at me sharply. "You didn't laugh."

"Why should I?" I say. "It's much too serious. I mean, I want to change things too, but not that way."

She fishes out some chewing-gum and offers me some. "You know," she tells me, "it's funny. That day you came to my class at primary school, we knew we'd be best friends. It was almost as if we've been best friends for ages…"

"Yes. Ages," I say slowly.

THE TIME TREE
by Enid Richemont

The tall tree in the park is Rachel and Joanna's special place.

It's Anne's too. So it's hardly surprising that the three girls meet up there – except for the fact that Anne was born over four hundred years ago!

"A very unusual ghost story." *Books*

"An enchanting and imaginative story, which will give modern children an idea of how it must have felt to be a child of the Elizabethan age." *The Lady*

THE PITS
by Lesley Howarth

Gang warfare in 7650 BC.

Things weren't so different back in the late Stone Age. The weather may have been colder but, as the ghost of Broddy Brodson will tell you, human behaviour was pretty much the same. And he should *know*. For Broddy was a member of the Axes gang that fought off the Pits for control of the sandpits that last, crazy, turbulent summer. He *knew* Ma Fingers, Treak the Bedeviller, Vert and Hayta, 'Viger Wildgoose, Cud, Eels, Argos, Arf... And now he's going to tell you the whole, incredible story!

"This is a sparky, humorous story, with a fast-moving plot... Lesley Howarth thinks big, and this is a big, challenging book."
Gilllian Cross,
The Times Educational Supplement

FIRE, BED AND BONE
by Henrietta Branford

The year is 1381 and unrest is spreading like plague.

England's peasants are tired of the hardship and injustice they suffer at the hands of harsh landlords. Rebellion is in the air, bringing dramatic and violent upheaval to the lives of families like Rufus, Comfort and their children – and even to dogs, like the old hunting bitch, who is the narrator of this unforgettable tale.

Winner of the Guardian Children's Fiction Prize and the Smarties Book Bronze Award, this extraordinary story depicts the tumult and tragedy of the Peasants' Revolt through the eyes, ears and nose of a dog.

THE PECULIAR POWER OF TABITHA BROWN
by Mary Hooper

"I looked down at myself. I saw black fur. I saw paws. And I knew immediately what had happened."

Tabitha Brown is surprised to learn she's been left a cat cushion in Great-aunt Mitzi's will. But soon, the true nature of her aunt's legacy becomes clear. Landing on her feet, Tabitha realizes she has inherited a peculiar and extraordinary power – and she quickly sets about making good use of it!

Intriguing and highly enjoyable, Mary Hooper's story is guaranteed to make you purr.

WHATEVER HAPPENED TO KATY-JANE?
by Jean Ure

Waking in hospital after a road accident, Katy-Jane quickly realizes that something is not right; in fact, many things are wrong. The strange mousy woman by her bedside claims to be her mum; but her mum died over a year ago.

She has different friends too, and different likes and interests – she even looks different. And yet she feels the same. How can she be Katy-Jane and not Katy-Jane? Whatever can have happened to her? And, most important of all, will she ever again be the person she once was?

Jean Ure's gripping story is full of mystery and suspense.

THE HOLLOW LAND
by Jane Gardam

"Nine stories, rich in character and incident, combine to form a mini saga of two families – one local to the Cumbrian fells, one 'incomers' from London... The writing is individual, observant, funny: a celebration of a landscape and its people."
Books For Keeps

"Authentic gold in every syllable... A book for readers, for people – of whatever age."
Junior Bookshelf

"A remarkable book." *The Times*

"Not to be missed." *The Guardian*

Winner of the Whitbread Children's Novel Award

MORE WALKER PAPERBACKS
For You to Enjoy

☐ 0-7445-6072-1   *The Time Tree*
by Enid Richemont   £3.99

☐ 0-7445-4347-9   *Twice Times Danger*
by Enid Richemont   £3.99

☐ 0-7445-4767-9   *The Pits*
by Lesley Howarth   £3.99

☐ 0-7445-5484-5   *Fire, Bed and Bone*
by Henrietta Branford   £3.99

☐ 0-7445-6399-2   *The Peculiar Power of*
Tabitha Brown
by Mary Hooper   £3.99

☐ 0-7445-4774-1   *Whatever Happened*
to Katy-Jane?
by Jean Ure   £3.99

☐ 0-7445-6065-9   *The Hollow Land*
by Jane Gardam   £3.99